Heavenly Revenge

By: Angelina Wilson

Acknowledgements

I truly want to give all the glory and honor to God. This is my fifth piece of work and I feel completely blessed. As always, I have to give my mother; Yvonne Johnson thanks, for without her there would be no me. Thank you, for life, as well as believing in me. I love you. To my Fiancé, Nick Levick. Thank you for pushing me, for helping me stay focused. I appreciate you more than you'll ever know. I love you. To my beautiful daughter's Nic'Keya and A'zyiah Levick, Mommy loves you both, you both don't understand how just being who you are pushes me every day. Everything I do is for you two. To my step son little Nick and my step daughter I'zaiya, I love you both, and I'm glad God has placed you in my life. To all my supporters, to everyone who has picked up any work I have published, I just want to thank you so much. Niagara Falls N.Y. I love y'all, the support from day one has been incredible. Thank you all so much for the love and support you all have shown.

Table of Contents

Introduction

I don't have no love story to tell,
No good times or make-believe fairy tales.
I was never rocked as a baby; never heard lullaby's,
I was left in my crib no one heard my cries.
How could your own mother be the reason for your black eyes?
As I got older, I had to fight to survive.
My mother on drugs, daddy a goner,
All I had was me, I was always a loner.
My name is Heavenly but all I know is hell,
How the fuck do you put your child up for sale.
How do you hold me hostage, afraid I'd tell?
My innocence had to be worth more than a crack pipe,
You had to hear me in the other room putting up a fight.
How long do I have to be a victim of my mother's sins?
How many times do I have to endure being raped over and over again?

My name is Heavenly and this is how the story of my revenge begins.

CHAPTER 1
Born in hell

Weighing in at 4 pounds 7ounces, I made my grand appearance into the world on April 1st. It was a rainy, spring morning. I was tiny, but my lungs were fully developed. I cried nonstop, as the doctors cleaned me off. One of the nurses had the privilege of cutting my umbilical cord that connected me to my evil mother Zora. No one else was in the room, Zora slept with so many people I guess my father was a mystery, so she says. Today was supposed to be a special day. But to Zora, nothing was special about today at all. She went seven months without proper prenatal care, her crack habit was more of her concern than I was.

"Congratulations on your baby girl," the doctor uttered while smiling at Zora. Doctor Franco warm wrinkled fingers, held me tight, as he bent down to place me on Zora's chest before making his way out of the room. Looking down at me, Zora rolled her eyes at the sight of me lying on her. "Can one of y'all get this thing off me, I need to get up out of here." Nurse Evans and Nurse Thompson looked at Zora like she was crazy, they made their way to her bedside to take hold of me. "I think you may be going through postpartum depression ma'am, it's best if you'd just relax for the time being." Evans spoke softly, with sheer discomfort in her high pitched voice. Zora looked at the nurse briefly, "did you just tell me to relax?" "Lady are you out of your damn mind, I didn't plan on having this baby. Can't you see ain't no daddy in this room." Both nurses looked at each other with sorrow in their eyes, they knew my life would be far from normal. "How about you give her a middle name honey?" Thompson asked Zora, trying to shift the conversation and lessen the tension. "How about you give her one? I pushed her ass out, and gave her my great grandma name. I don't have time for this shit, I got stuff to do and places to be." Nurse Evans ran out the room as tears filled her eyes, her small frame waltzed right out the room bumping into another nurse. She never met anyone like Zora before. She knew she had to call Child

Protective Services; this was the part of the job she hated. She continued to sob, as the other nurse helped her to her feet. She knew that not only was there something mentally wrong with Zora, but her lab results showed drugs in both of our systems.

Nurse Thompson stayed in the room with Zora, she wanted to make sure I would be taken care of properly. "Hey, I think I have a middle name. What do you think about Rayne? It's spelled R-A-Y-N-E but pronounced Rain". "Heavenly Rayne Shine, I think it's a beautiful name" Thompson challenged, as she tried to get Zora to oblige. "Chile, I done told you I don't give a damn, you want to be her daddy too? Shit, we need some damn child support" Zora spat harshly. All Thompson could do was shake her head, she knew there was no getting through to this woman. Zora didn't care that she just gave birth to me, she even refused to fill out the birth certificate.

Nurse Evans stood outside of the room, she despised Zora because this situation hit too close to home for her. Evans wanted a child, she and her husband had been trying to have a baby. It wasn't until last month when she found out she would never be able to conceive. You could tell she adored me, she sang to me and rocked me to sleep whenever she could. If only she could take me home with her, she would take really good care of me. However, in the real world things didn't actually work like that. Once CPS was contacted Zora was forced to go into rehab, that would be the only way she would be allowed to take me home. That was her least concern though, she was more worried about jail. If she didn't complete the program, they would arrest her ass. Now we all know; Zora wasn't built for jail. Anything that kept her away from that glass pipe, she didn't want any parts of it. The sad thing was, all she had to do was seven days. 7 funky ass days for birthing a crack baby, 7 mothafuckin days for child neglect. After that, they would allow her to be released. She would be able to take me home, without any further incident. Those seven days at the hospital, was the most love I got since being pushed out of Zora's nasty stank coochie. The nurses held me, rocked me and made me feel safe. I spent the first week of my life with complete strangers, looking at different faces every shift change. I was feeling myself getting attached, especially to nurse Evans. Whenever she held me life seemed to feel so much better. My tiny heart would race every time I saw her, when she held me I would fall asleep instantaneously. The love I felt was real, compared to the love I was shown from my own mother. From the day I arrived in this pernicious world, I knew the name Heavenly would only mean the exact opposite.

I had an older brother named Zoe, he was Zora's pride and joy. Her first born son was like her God, her savior and her meal ticket. I was only a mistake, Zora had me ten years after Zoe and she was already showing me she wanted no parts of me. She already hated my existence, my presence alone caused her melancholy, she was sickened by her unwanted creation.

Today would be the day I was scheduled to go home, Zora had to pick me up from the hospital. The nurses had purchased me a car seat, CPS bought clothing, formula and diapers. They knew she wouldn't be buying anything; she had nothing and didn't plan on getting anything for me.

Why did God curse me from the seed? I was born with everything against me before birth, I already knew I was destined for failure. I was born on April fool's day, what a coincidence right? I guess the joke was on me.

CHAPTER 2
From bad to worse

"**Z**oe, don't be out there getting into no shit. You know we depend on you baby boy." Zora called out after Zoe, he was fired up about someone stealing his money. He brought Zora her usual $1,000, he made it his business to look after us. Zora pranced around the living room, wearing a skimpy skin tight two-piece romper. Even though she was a crack addict, she carried herself very well. Her nails and hair were always done, she wore 22-inch blonde bundles faithfully. Her hair went well with her light brown skin tone and oval brown eyes, that turned chinky every time she smiled. Her round face was still full of life, she had a body to kill for. Nothing about Zora was fake, she could definitely give Jennifer Lopez a run for her booty. Zoe would always get into fights about Zora, everyone wanted the chance to lay up with her and of course she would open her legs for the right price. She would either get paid with money or drugs. Everyone knew she had a habit, but they also knew she had that fire pussy. Niggas would say her pussy would clap right on there dick, they even nicknamed her coochie "snap crack." Shit was bizarre in the hood, niggas thought fucking crackheads was the new lingo. Zoe knew she was a closet junkie, but that didn't stop him from giving her money. As long as she took care of me, he was fine knowing that she wasn't strung out. Before Zoe left the house every day, he made sure he kissed my forehead and hugged me tight. He would play with my pigtails, pinch my cheeks and give me a few dollars. I loved my big brother; his love was all the love I felt in that gruesome apartment we called home.

Today I turned five years old, Zoe made sure each year my birthday was special. Little did he know, all I needed was him to be around for it to be special. This year, he bought me a gold chain and a matching bracelet set. On my necklace where two angel wings, of course they went well with my name. My brother went all out for me, in my eyes he was my daddy. Zoe was gone the majority of the time; so, he didn't know what was going on in Zora's house. He didn't know Zora was beating on me every chance she got, just because she felt like it. I always thought she was jealous of the love Zoe had for me, her only son didn't see her as the main priority any more. Before I came into the picture she got all the money, time and attention from him. Now he made sure I was taken care of first, and she despised it. Zoe was a corner boy for Murder Max, some say he made over $5,000 a day. He showed love to everyone, so for someone to steal from him; had him furious. "On God, I'm gone kill one of these niggas." I could hear Zoe fuming from the front porch, so I made my way outside to try to cheer him up. Liberty Square, also known as the Pork and Bean project was lit. Everyone was outside on this warm April afternoon, as the smell of barbecue food filled the air. It was a shooting every day out here, sometimes two and three times a day. I grew accustomed to the sound of gunshots, they no longer scared me but it gave me the ability to identify what kind of gun was being fired.

"Heavenly get down," Zoe panicked while trying to push me back into the house. Shots from a 32 semi-automatic Smith and Wesson could be heard, as innocent bystanders yelled out in agony. It was insane how a 5 year old girl could identify a gun, just from the sound of it. 7 rounds whizzed in our direction, like the bullets had our names on them. Zoe's body laid on top of mine, as he shielded me from the gun fire. Once the chaos stopped, screams could be heard in the distance. I was still trapped under Zoe, too afraid to move and too terrified to breath. "What the fuck you do to my baby? Get your stupid ass up Heavenly." Zora screamed at me like I was just another kid on the block, she lifted Zoe's body and cried out as she saw blood covering the porch. Blood seeped from every hole in Zoe's body, my little hands tried to put pressure on Zoe's wounds but Zora pushed me away forcefully. My all white dress was also covered in my brothers' blood, I stood still not registering what just occurred. "Somebody help me, my son's been shot." Zora rocked Zoe's limp body back and forth, she sat holding him with tears cascading down her face. Hearing siren's getting close, Zora did the unthinkable. She ran her own son's pockets, taking all of his money and the little bit of drugs he had left on him, stuffing it all into her bra. Her Oscar performance left me amazed at how trifling she really was, but yet I wasn't surprised at all. I've seen a lot of things Zora did, as a child I usually stayed in a child's place. Even if I wanted to say something, I knew Zora would beat my ass.

The paramedics finally arrived, they worked on Zoe hastily while placing him on a stretcher. "Please save my baby, he's all I got." Zora begged, as she cried hysterically putting on another performance. "Who might this little beauty be?" A female officer walked up to me, while wrapping a blanket around me. "Are you this child's mother also?" The cop asked Zora. Looking back at me, Zora rolled her eyes. "Can't you see I'm grieving my got damn son, he may not even make it, but you're standing here asking stupid ass questions."

"Ma'am, this little girl is pretty shaken up. I'm just trying to help, she's going to need support and maybe even counseling." The cop was really nice, but Zora wasn't trying to hear shit. All she cared about was Zoe and if we lost him she knew she lost her income, her lifestyle and her provider. I couldn't believe my brother was fighting for his life, he saved mine without any hesitation. After working on Zoe for about ten minutes, the paramedics pulled off. Zora and I were taken to the hospital in a cop car, she didn't say anything to me the entire ride.

Once we arrived, the waiting room was filled to capacity. So many people were victims of today's drive by shootings, some were already told their loved one didn't make it.

"I'm looking to speak with the family of Zoe Shine." The doctor came out looking around, Zora jumped up and walked towards him hurriedly. I followed a few steps behind knowing I shouldn't have, but I needed to know if Zoe was alright. "I'm so sorry ma'am, Mr. Shine was DOA. Our team worked hard to revive him but unfortunately we were unsuccessful, the amount of blood he lost was a factor in his death." Zora just stared blankly, then she let out a gut wrenching cry. "Not my baby, what am I going to do without my Zoe."

"I'm very sorry for your loss ma'am." The doctor dismissed himself, he made his way towards the other families. I sat there next to Zora, knowing she wouldn't care that I was still in complete shock. My big brother died on my 5th birthday.

"This is all your fault little girl, you should have stayed your fast ass in the house. Because of you, my fucking son is dead." Looking up at Zora, I could see the hatred she had in her eyes for me. I cried silently, wishing it was me instead of Zoe. "Would you like a ride home ma'am?" The female cop from earlier asked Zora, she must have heard that Zoe didn't make it. "I don't need no damn ride, where the hell you come from anyhow?" The cop ignored Zora's ignorance and made her way over to me. Bending down, she tucked something into my pocket. "If you ever need any help, please call the number on the card." She whispered in my ear, before standing back up and walking away. I knew from today on, things with this bitch I call my mother; would only go from bad to worse.

CHAPTER 3
Saying Goodbye

*A*pril 6th, five days after my birthday, I sat in the front pew of Liberty City Church of Christ, witnessing Zoe lying in a casket. For some reason, I tuned everything out while everyone around me spoke amongst themselves. The unpleasant cries, the fake homies and the chicks who claimed they loved him, left an uneasy sensation in the pit of my stomach. Then there was the devil herself, Zora. She sat in silence, as people approached her to give their condolences. Rocking an all-black dress, with a black sun hat, her entire demeanor screamed a mother in mourning to everyone besides me. Rocking back and forth in her seat, her face was wet with tears. The church was packed, every seat was filled. Standing up in the back of the church, where different street sets. Members of NW 79th, wore white. NW 27th, wore blue. It was crazy how so many different people came out and showed love, setting all their differences aside they made sure Zoe was laid to rest peacefully. Even though Zoe was a corner boy, who ran with the NW 35th district; at his age he grew up to respect everyone on the block. In return, they respected my brother, so whoever was responsible for his death, had a death wish.

Everyone from the 35th district wore red, including Zoe laying in his casket. After a few people spoke highly of Zoe, I made my way up toward the altar to speak. Zora twisted up her face and gave me the deadliest stare, but I didn't care how she felt. I walked right past her and grabbed the mic. All eyes were on me, some people even whispered how small and cute I was. While others looked on in shock, as I decided to wear the white dress covered in Zoe's dried up blood.

Taking a deep breath, I began to read what I wrote. "Five days ago, my life changed. Five days ago was my fifth birthday. I haven't been able to grasp the fact that Zoe is gone, or even understand why. Today I stand here before you all, wearing the same dress I wore when Zoe's body collapsed on me. He saved my life; not knowing he would lose his. He so selflessly protected me, more than anyone else ever had.

I didn't get to choose a new dress to wear today, or new shoes, or even a new hairdo. You want to know why? Because I've been blamed for the death of my only brother." Whispers escaped the mouths of many, then silence fell throughout the church. Zora's facial expression told me she would deal with me later, I already knew that though. So, I continued. "Zoe was more than just my brother, he was my hero and my best friend. I'm the forbidden child, the mistake of my family but Zoe didn't treat me like that." Murmurs could be heard throughout the church once again, many people looked over at Zora giving her disapproving glares. "Before I step down, I just want you to know I love you Zoe. I wish we could trade places, but God had better plans for you. Until we meet again, please protect me big brother. Goodbye Zoe." Everyone stood up and clapped, as I made my way back to my seat. There wasn't a dry eye in the church, I wanted everyone to know the truth.

Pastor King had a few words for the people, he talked highly of Zoe, he knew firsthand that Zoe was troubled but he also knew he was a good kid. Before the funeral ended, a short black lady began to sing a solo, which only made everyone cry again.

Six of Zoe's trusted friends were honored to be his pallbearers, they walked him outside to be placed in the hearse. I cried, knowing I would never see his face again and reality was just setting in. This was a different kind of hurt, this hurt more than the beatings from Zora. I'd take a beating everyday from her, if I could just have my Zoe back. "Heavenly, get your stupid ass over here. I should make you walk home, since you tried to make me look stupid in the house of God." I just ignored her and made my way into the car she sat in. Murder Max sat in the driver seat, avoiding eye contact with me. I knew Zora just got a quick fix; her eyes were glossy as hell. If Zoe was alive, Max knew damn well he wouldn't disrespect him like that. It's crazy how people do you once you're dead and gone, the disrespect was real and Zoe wasn't even six feet under yet. The smell in the car was awful, it smelled like burning plastic; a smell that I grew to learn was crack. "Do you have a problem, you fucking murderer?" Zora yelled at me, as white pieces of spit appeared in the corners of her mouth. "C'mon, take it easy on the kid." Max spoke up in my defense, as he looked at me in the rearview mirror with lustful eyes. Tears welled up in my eyes, but I refused to let them fall. Zora would love to see me cry, but I held it all inside refusing to give her any satisfaction.

Max dropped us off at home, as I made my way to the front porch, a sharp pain shot up my spine. Zora kicked me so hard in the back, I fell face first on the ground. "Get up bitch, you ain't seen nothing yet." Zora threatened, with a mischievous grin across her face, as she stepped right over my tiny body. Picking myself up, I looked around in embarrassment. Max eyes locked with mine, before he drove off he blew me a kiss. I had no idea what his intentions were, and I sure wasn't trying to find out either. Why would a grown ass man, blow a 5 year old a kiss anyway, that way some perverted shit I thought.

Weeks went by, and Zora was getting high more than usual. You could tell Zoe's death took its toll on her. Instead of tending to my needs, she entertained the neighborhood crack heads. Every night there was a party in the house, I stayed in my room away from the chaos almost all of the time. Zora would leave me home, while she went out and strolled the corners. She was now into selling her body for pennies, since her funds were running low and she didn't have anyone else to supply her needs. Sometimes I'd run down the street to grab some chips and a drink, one thing Zoe always taught me was to make sure I always had money, because of his teachings I always had a little something hidden.

One particular night, Zora let some crackhead by the name of Biggs stay in our home. I was so afraid to leave, I didn't want to wake him up. I was so hungry and I hadn't eaten all day, against my better judgement I made my way towards the living room where he slept. "Where are you going beautiful?" Biggs' raspy voice startled me. I turned back around towards my room, but he stood up almost instantly. My heart dropped, as this big black 6-foot man towered over me. Biggs grabbed my arm leaving his handprint, as he dragged me towards my room. I cried nonstop as snot ran from my nose, but he didn't care at all. He shoved me on the floor, since all I had was two padded mats and a pillow, Zora didn't even think I was good enough for a blow up bed. He unbuckled his pants in a hurry and let them fall to the floor, Biggs pulled a big ugly looking snake from his boxers. Aggressively, he pulled down my pants. His snake made its way inside of my vagina, after several minutes of him forcing himself in me. The pain shot up my stomach, while blood formed below me. "Stop kicking me girl, I'm turning you into my woman." I couldn't believe this man was raping me, I couldn't believe he thought I wanted to be his woman. I was still a kid, nothing on my body was developed, my nipples hadn't even popped out yet. I was five years old when my innocence was snatched from me.

Hearing Zora's voice gave me a sign of hope, never in a million years did I ever think I'd be happy to hear her voice. But tonight I needed her, I wanted her to save me from Biggs.

Zora pushed my room door open, shock crossed her face as Biggs body rocked on top of mine. Biggs seemed startled at first, but Zora smiled at him. "Nigga is you out of your got damn mind, that's my mothafuckin child you fucking." Biggs began to speak, but Zora cut him off. "Now you no ain't shit free, after you get that nut, you're gonna pay me." Zora walked out the room, slamming the door behind her. She left me in the room with Biggs, I closed my eyes and endured the pain he was inflicting between my legs. When Zora walked in, I just knew she was finna fuck Biggs up, but her eyes gave it away. Instead of fighting for her daughter, money signs flashed before her eyes and that was all she wrote.

CHAPTER 4
Trouble Everywhere

No matter what I couldn't get a break, trouble at home led to trouble at school. Trouble at school, led to trouble at the group home. I had a hard time focusing and of course everyone picked on me for obvious reasons. The popular girls ridiculed me, while the boys loved my figure but were too cmbarrassed to speak to me.

At the age of fifteen, my body was overly developed. I had a feeling this was the result of being raped, since it happened on more than fifty different occasions. 10 years ago, when Zora walked in on Biggs, she made it a constant habit . She sold my body from age five, until age thirteen. It only stopped because I began to run away, if I wasn't around she couldn't make any money. Zora didn't want shit to do with me, so after I ran away 2 years ago she placed me in a group home. They made sure my ass attended school, which I hated with a passion. I was in ninth grade, attending Miami Northern Senior high school. Every day, I was in some kind of trouble. The girls at this school fucked with me in the bathroom, they tried to cut my hair and intimidate me. The boys tried to secretly fuck me in the auditorium, but I wasn't having that. I was a cute, bright skin girl. Many people mistook me for being a white girl. My skin complexion was a bit on the white side especially during the winter months, but anyone with common sense could tell I was mixed with something. What I was mixed with, was up for debate. Zora didn't know who my daddy was, so I would never know either. I had long brownish honey blonde hair that flowed past my butt. My golden-brown eyes had a set of naturally arched eyebrows. My perky set of breasts were only in a B cup, but my round plump ass was perfect. With all my perfections, of course there were many imperfections. My clothes were raggedy, my sneakers were old and I wore the same hairstyle every single day. Many of the girls in the school taunted me, so I was always left defending myself. I was far from a punk, fighting was nothing to me, I had to fight my whole life. However, the bitches at my school where all talk they really didn't want no smoke with me.

"You still didn't wash your clothes, walking around looking like yesterday." Saharra chuckled, as she and her friend Kacey walked past me, it wouldn't be Saharra if she didn't have something to say. She was the head cheerleader of the school, as well as the most popular girl. She looked average, but her popularity is what made her. Standing at about 5'9, she had caramel toned skin, with black hair that reached her shoulders, she usually wore it in a bob. Her oval shaped brown eyes were always covered in eye shadow, with a round set of full lips, that curled everytime she smirked.

"Are you still mad, since obviously your boyfriend likes my dirty ass?" Rolling my eyes, I began walking to my third period class. "Girl, Chaz wouldn't give you the time of day. My boyfriend knows what he got and your dusty ass ain't it," she laughed. "Girl, get the fuck out my face." I snapped, while dismissing myself from her fuckery. Saharra knew how to get under my skin, she always made it her business to fuck with me any chance she got. Kacey was her best friend, I knew she only wanted to fit in, so she tagged right along with Saharra.

"Heavenly, where are you going?" I was already familiar with the deep baritone voice, so I knew it was Chaz. He was the quarterback of the school, he was popular also. All the girls wanted him, but Saharra had him already.

"Boy, what do you want?" Taken back, by my ignorant response, Chaz just shook his head.

"Damn, it's like that?"

"Yes, it's like that, now go chase after your little girlfriend. I don't have time for this shit, I need to go to class."

"His little girlfriend is right here," Saharra spoke up, as she made her way towards us. "Chaz, why are you even entertaining this dusty little bitch?" Saharra looked at Chaz, then her eyes landed back on me. "Man, she bumped into me and then started talking to me, after she almost made me drop my stuff," Chaz lies fell right from his tongue. He tried his best to make up any lie, so Saharra didn't get mad at him. "Don't you ever let me catch you talking to this peasant, we have nothing in common with her except this school." Chaz reached for Saharra's hand, she handed him a fountain drink. "I'm good babe, I'm not thirsty" Chaz told her. Saharra smiled, while looking directly at me. "I know you're not, but she is. So why don't you give her thirsty ass something to drink," Saharra provoked him, as speculators watched in excitement. Chaz was hesitant at first, but with a growing crowd instigating some action, he listened to what Saharra asked him to do. Walking over to me, he poured an entire cup of soda over my head. Everyone had their phone's drawn recording the incident, hoping to get the most views on Youtube. My hair was sticky and my white shirt was now brown, I was embarrassed as everyone looked at me laughing. I decided to skip class and made my way out of the school. Curfew for the group home was 8 o'clock. So, I wasn't going straight there. With so much on my mind I decided to take a walk, walking led me to an unknown neighborhood. All I really needed was some air to clear my mind, I wanted to be alone with no one to interrupt my thoughts.

"What chu doing in my hood, I think you might be lost?" I was startled by a raspy voice behind me, I turned around quickly to see who the man was. I'm just walking, I ain't bothering nobody" I replied. "The only folks who come through here, are dealers or prostitutes. Now I know you ain't selling no work, so you must be selling pussy," He laughed. I didn't find his ignorance funny, so I continued on my way. I guess that only added insult to injury, the man was furious that I didn't acknowledge him. He grabbed me by my arm, digging his nails into my skin. "Yo, Biggs take it easy." Another man shouted as he walked towards us, trying to keep everything cordial. I almost pissed myself when he said Biggs, I knew he looked familiar; I would never forget his face. Biggs was the same man who raped me in Zora's house, when I was just five years old. He didn't look the same, but there were some features I'd never forget. As soon as the other guy told him to let me go, I took off running down the street refusing to look back. I was out of breath but I didn't care, I had to get away as quickly as possible.

After running for almost five minutes, I sat down at a bus stop to catch my breath. I had to get back to the group home, otherwise I would have a curfew violation.

"Beep, beep."

A car horn got my attention, but with the dark tent I couldn't see who was inside. The driver rolled his window down and to my surprise it was Murder Max. I hadn't seen him in about five years. After Zoe died, he didn't come around too often. From what I heard, he was picked up on some drug charges and went up North. "You gonna act like you don't know me?" Max yelled from across the street. I stood up, and walked towards his car. I guess getting a ride was better than waiting for a bus, I hated to get in the car with this creep, but I really had no choice. "You out here looking rough girl, what's going on with you?" Max asked with concern. "Where should I start from Max? Should I start all the way back to when Zoe was murdered, how Zora ain't want shit to do with me, or should I tell you about this fucking group home, or maybe school? Of course I'm out here looking crazy, I ain't got shit or nobody." I was yelling at Max unknowingly, as I released myself from years of built up emotions. "Damn Heavenly, calm down. I didn't mean it like that." Max tried his best to console me, not understanding why I took my frustration out on him.

"Can you please take me to the group home? It's off of Martin Luther king Blvd."

"Yeah, I got you." Max replied just above a whisper. We drove in silence, for most of the ride. Finally, Max decided to try to redeem himself. "Listen Heavenly, I know shit has been crazy in your life, but I'm here now. Yo brother was like my brother, when he died a part of me died too. I always wanted to look at you like a little sister, but I always wanted more." "When you were younger, I told you I'd be back in ten years for you. I'm here now and I want to make you mine." I looked at Max like he was crazy, he ignored me and continued talking. "I know I'm way older than you but I feel we belong together," he concluded. "If Zoe was alive, you no damn well he wouldn't go for this," I told him. "Well he ain't alive, so who's gonna stop us?" Max could see what he said got to me, as a lone tear escaped the corner of my eye. "I'm sorry, that came out wrong," he said apologetically. I wiped my face immediately, angry that I let him see me cry. "Here, take this money. Go find you something nice, I'll pick you up tomorrow or something." He handed me a wad of bills, along with his phone number. I took them and placed them in my pocket. Thanks for the ride, I gave him a quick hug and made my way out of his car.

"Was that Max?" Vonie, one of the chicks who worked at the group home asked. "Yeah, that was him." I replied while making my way past her. She knew everything, about everybody. All Vonie did was gossip all day, she was better than the newspapers. "I didn't know he was out of jail; I use to fuck with him to," she blurted out. "Girl, I don't fuck with him, he used to be close to my family."

"Oh, well none of that matters anyhow, after he killed that boy he ain't been the same," she said while shaking her head. "What the fuck are you talking about Vonie?" She began telling me a story. "This was about ten years ago, you were a baby then, so you wouldn't remember." "Max skipped town after the shooting, then he ended up going to jail for some other shit."

"Ten years ago? Are you sure it was ten years ago?" I quizzed her. "Yeah, I'm sure. I was living in the pork and beans project when it happened, I tell this story so many damn times, but you no these cops round here won't solve no murder."

"Ten years ago, I was living out there too." I told her. "Oh, for real? well back then, the young boy had to be like 15 or 16, but I'm not too certain of his exact age though." "Well do you know his name?" I was hoping she knew it, she knew every damn thing else. "Nope, all I know is that the boy's mama loved the hell out of him, even though she was a crackhead she took it hard when he died." "Matter of fact, I think her name was Zorey or Zorah, something like that." "She's still around the way, looking crazy and smoked out as ever." A sense of dizziness overcame me, I couldn't catch my breath, I felt light headed. A nasty taste formed in my mouth, before I could react everything inside of my stomach was now splattered on the ground. "Damn Heavenly, are you okay? You almost got that shit all over my uniform." Running to my room, I left Vonie outside without an explanation. I couldn't believe what she said or if it had any truth to it, I really didn't know what to think at this point. Why would Max want to kill Zoe? What would be his motive? I thought to myself. I had so many questions, but nothing made any sense. I'd have to play my cards right and stay close to Max. If all was true, Max would be number one on my list. Then after him I was going to get Biggs fat ass. I knew what he looked like now and where he hung out. He would never know what hit his ass, neither one of these niggas would.

CHAPTER 5
Who's That?

$\mathcal{E}$veryone stopped as I walked by, heads were turning and mouths were dropping. I made it my business, to go purchase me some new clothes. With the $500 Max gave me, I went out and got a few cute outfits. Today I decided to wear a pink and white mini skirt with a white button up shirt, two of the buttons were undone because my boobs were busting out. On my feet I had the newly released hot pink Air Maxes, with long white and pink striped socks that went up to my knees. My hair was crimped and I wore a light foundation. "Who is that?" I heard a few people say, the boys drooled at the sight of me but their girlfriends cringed. I walked right to my locker, absorbing all of the attention I was getting. "Holy shit, you look good as hell." Jackson, one of the school's football running backs, flirted as he walked closely by me. I rolled my eyes at Jackson, then started making my way to class, he never liked me the least bit. Before I opened my classroom door, Chaz stopped me dead in my tracks. "Hey Heavenly, you look beautiful today." I tried to stop myself from blushing, but I secretly liked Chaz. Several people walked by us and out of nowhere Chaz started shouting causing an unnecessary scene. "Just because you cleaned up a little bit, don't mean I want you." My face turned a light shade of red, it was only obvious Saharra was right behind me. Chaz must have seen her and decided to flip the script on me. Saharra smiled, as she walked over to Chaz. "Once trash, always trash. Just because you clean yourself for one day, doesn't mean you're no longer garbage." "Remember, trash only gets picked up once a week." Saharra continued to cause more drama while looking me up and down, secretly checking me out. Grabbing Chaz's hand, they both headed down the hallway. Chaz looked back at me momentarily, before turning back around. If I didn't hate him just a little bit, I really hated his ass now but I hated Saharra even more. They would both pay for how they treated me, I always liked Chaz, now I despised the ground he walked on. With everyone still out in the halls, I finally made it to English class.

Everyone talked amongst themselves, of course I was the topic of discussion. "Damn is that Heavenly?" "Who is dat?" "She's probably still dirty." I couldn't even focus, everyone had something to say like I wasn't right there.

We had an English exam today, as much as I wanted to walk out I stayed. It took about an hour for everyone to complete the exam. Once everyone was done, the teacher allowed everyone to do whatever they pleased for the remaining time we had left of class. Some classmates took their phones out, while others got on the school computers. I sat at my desk, minding my business twirling my pencil. I was so ready to get out of here, it was Friday and I was allowed to stay out until ten tonight.

"Oh shit, look at this." Everyone in the class started gathering around Billy, he was always the first to get any information going on in the school. Not too soon after, everyone's phones began going off, everyone except mine because I didn't have one. Billy walked towards the computer; he expanded a Youtube video. On the video, you could see Chaz pouring the drink over my head and Saharra laughing hysterically. After that clip ended, you could see me alone changing in the locker room. Someone had recorded me undressing, while I changed. "Look at Miss. Bloody panties." Saharra's voice was clear as day; of course she was responsible for all of this. A few weeks ago, I got my period unexpectedly. Unbeknownst to me, I was being recorded while I was in the bathroom stall. I grabbed my books as my hands started shaking, I left the classroom hoping to make it to the exit without any further insults.

"Bloody panties, Bloody Panties." Saharra was chanting in the hallway, everyone else following her lead. They continued to shout bloody panties, over and over again. I made my way down the hall, Saharra was right on my heels like I stole something.

"You thought you could change your reputation huh? You'll forever be, dirty ass Heavenly."

"Fuck you Saharra, get out of my way" I yelled. "Or what? What are you going to do if I don't bloody panties?" Saharra laughed, which caused everyone else to join in laughter. I pushed her out of my face, she stumbled backwards with a wicked grin. Saharra ran towards me, with her fist balled up. I grabbed for my bra; my razor was tapped inside. Saharra wailed on me, punching me non-stop. I was finally able to grab my razor, I swung it wildly. For a moment I blacked out, I screamed as I continued to slash Saharra all over her body. "Somebody grab that crazy bitch, she's going to kill her." I could hear Kacey yelling, I wanted to slash her face too. But it was too late, the school security was running down the hall ready to take action. My hands were covered in blood, and my nose was leaking blood from Saharra punching me. With everyone in the hall, I knew it would probably be nearly impossible to escape. I tried anyhow, I ran full speed down the hall. No one tried to stop me, so I ran right out the door. The fat ass security guard almost caught me, but he wasn't able to keep up with me. I kept running down the street until I came across a pay phone, I dialed the only number I knew.

"Who this?" Max answered on the first ring. "Hey Max, it's Heavenly. I got an emergency and I really could use your help, I put a little emphasis on help."

"What do you need?" Max asked, sounding a little pleased that I called. I gave him my location and told him I needed him to hurry. I ended the call and walked on the side of a building, I didn't want anyone to see me. I had to stay out of sight, knowing that I just assaulted someone at school. I was almost certain; they already called the cops. Even though it was self-defense, they would still charge me for using a weapon. I dropped the bloody razor into a drain, and placed my other one in my mouth.

After waiting about twenty minutes, Max pulled up. I ran out of hiding and hopped into his whip. "Damn Heavenly, what the fuck happened to you?" Max asked, while looking at my blood covered clothing. "I'm good, just get me up out of here," I told him. Max drove for almost an hour, before we pulled up to a two-story house. The house was beautiful, we were in the better parts of Miami.

"Where are we?"

"Well, I thought it was a good idea to bring you to my home. I mean, where else was I gonna take you," he replied.

Looking at Max, I just gave an approving look, I didn't have the right to complain. I really needed him, beings that I had no place to go. I couldn't go back to the group home, or they would turn my ass in. Now was my chance to get in good with Max, it was a game well worth playing. "Make yourself at home Heavenly, I'm going to take a shower." Max yelled out from the hallway. I went right to the living room, and turned on the television. After about five minutes of flicking through the channels, I got bored and curiosity was getting the best of me. I made my way to the kitchen, then towards the back of the house. He was taking his time upstairs, so I began snooping around. I had to give it to him, for a man, his house was nice. It was cozy, but you could tell a man lived there, it had no woman's touch at all. He had 2 big screens on the wall, a pool table in the middle of the floor, and a bar off to the side. I continued to lurk, until I reached his den. I went inside his cabinets, just being nosey. I made my way over to a desk; a stack of papers were piled on it. A gold manila envelope caught my attention, so I pulled it from underneath all the distorted paperwork.

Dumping the contents out, my eyes must have deceived me. Inside was a $100,000 insurance policy, with Zoe's name written in big bold letters. The policy was taken out, two months before his death. Under that was an agreement, between Max and Zora. Zora promised to give Max $30,000. I continued to study the paperwork, I could tell which hand writing was his, since he wrote the letter. Reading out loud to myself what he wrote on paper, I was perplexed at what he'd written. "In the event that he does not receive his $30,000 for doing his part, he would use this paperwork as evidence against her. Which was stupid, because it would implicate his dumb ass to I thought. Knowing Max, he knew Zora wouldn't think that deep. I could not believe what I was reading, me being nosey just gave me the answer's I needed. My brother was murdered, because Zora wanted money. Not only that, but she paid his best friend to kill him. Hearing the shower turn off, made me realize I needed to get out of there. I ran back into the living room, acting as if I was there the entire time.

Moments later, Max came out with just a towel wrapped around his scrowney frame.

"You ready to give me some of that pussy?" Max smiled mischievously, while licking his lips. You'd think I was a piece of steak, the way he looked like he wanted to devour me. "Yes, I'm ready." I lied, but I began taking off my clothes contemplating my next move. "Alright then, come ride this dick." Max sat on the couch with his dick out, I wanted to throw up. His uncircumcised dick, was about 5 inches. After about three minutes of me fondling him, he instructed me to stand up since I refused to put his dick in my mouth. Max's head was tilted all the way back, as he entered inside of me. I wanted to scream but I remained calm, like I used to when I was a little girl. Max's eyes were closed, as he moaned loudly. I kissed him on his cheek softly, before spitting my razor out of my mouth.

"This is for my mothafuckin brother bitch," his eyes snapped open quickly but it was too late. I slashed his throat three times, before he even realized it. Blood poured from his throat, he fought to breathe while choking on his own blood. He laid limp with his pants around his ankles, his eyes bulged from the sockets. Making my way upstairs I took a quick shower, washing all signs of him off of me. I made my way into every room, searching for anything valuable. When I came across his safe, I knew I wouldn't be disappointed. Once the safe was open, from a key I found in his drawer, I was delighted. Stacks of money were lined up inside, along with two packages of weed, a pistol and some Jewelry. I placed everything into a backpack, including the agreement between him and Zora, then I made my way to the kitchen. I turned on the stove and poured cooking grease all over it. Within seconds the fire started, it began to spread throughout the house. I made my way out the back door, never once looking back.

CHAPTER 6
Time to Plot

*T*ears continued to fall down my face, I sat in a run down motel crying my eyes out. I couldn't believe they killed Zoe, he didn't deserve that shit. They always say, it's the ones that's close to you who would be the first to hurt you. I knew Zora was grimy, but damn her own fucking son. The same son who provided for her, the same son who gave her money day in and day out. My heart was crushed, I knew Vonie didn't have a reason to lie but to actually see for myself was devastating. It was a reason she told me that, I wonder if she knew who I was all along. Vonie was a drama queen, any way she could fuck someone's life up she would. I was tired of people fucking with me, to be honest I was just tired period.

Once I got myself together, I hid the money under the bed. There weren't too many hiding places in this small sized room,but I had to make it work. I had to settle for a cheap motel, that was my only option at this point since I was a minor. Trying to get a high class room would put me under the radar, I didn't need any more drama. These motels didn't care who rented them, as long as they got paid. The older bald head guy was happy, when I gave him enough money for the rest of the year. This would be my home for now, I had to play safe and be sure to play smart. I would make sure to find Zora, she had to get dealt with. I had to admit, it did feel good killing the mothafucka who killed Zoe, but Zora was responsible to and I couldn't let that slide. Everything happened so fast, I would have never thought I'd be capable of killing him so quickly. I probably would have been sleeping with the enemy, if it wasn't for Vonie running her big mouth.

Sitting down on the bed flicking through the channels, I found myself creating a plot. I grabbed a piece of paper and a pen, and started writing down the names of all the people who did me wrong. I already got Max out the way, now I had to find Biggs's ass again. I knew where to find him, but I also knew he wasn't no amateur either. I didn't know all the men who took advantage of me, but I was on a mission to find them. When Zora would let them rape me, she never said their names. I only knew Biggs, because he was always around. I started writing down every feature I could remember, the cologne they wore and any marks or scars that I could recall. Even though I didn't know their names, it wouldn't stop me from finding out who those perverts were. I guess no one was safe, I'd ruin every man's life, like they ruined mine with no remorse. No one gave a fuck about me, so I could care less about anyone at this point. Chaz, Saharra, Kacey, they would all feel my pain. I had one mission and one mission only. *REVENGE.*

"Everyone who caused me harm, fucked with my mind and abandoned me,

I'm comin' for you, two times worse than the pain you caused me.

Y'all turned me insane, bitch I'm warm blooded but cold hearted.

I'm comin with my razor blade, call me crazy, but this is something y'all started."

Being in this motel, had me going crazy. I would sit and write for hours, sometimes without eating because I was hungry for more than just food. I was finishing up one of my hate poems, writing was my escape from reality. I put my pen and notebook away and reached under the bed to grab the back pack.

The incident with Max happened over a week ago, I still haven't counted the money or opened the bag since I was paranoid. I began sorting out the bill's, when I was finished, I counted $15,000. I wasn't sure I counted correctly, so I counted again, that's when I realized I was really $15,000 richer. Excitement overwhelmed me; I tossed the money all over the room like cleo from set it off. I wish I had a friend though, someone who could help me spend this shit. But since I didn't, I would go treat myself since I did deserve it.

Getting off the bed, I taped the gun under the nightstand. I put the Jewelry and weed under the dresser, the safe in the room was too obvious so I didn't use it. I had to get myself together, my first stop would be the hair store. I wanted to change my hair color, and chop about five inches off my extremely long hair. After the first part of my experiment was complete, I wanted to get some contacts to enhance my change. My entire appearance would be completely different, there would be a new Heavenly in town.

I only had a few items of clothing to choose from, so I took a shower and got dressed. After showering I put on my pink Air Maxes, a pink and white striped shirt and some blue jeans. This outfit was the one I bought when Max gave me the $500. I never wore it, so I was looking fresh and feeling good. Putting my hair in a slick back ponytail, I made my way from the motel.

It took me 3 buses to get to the mall, I was already tired just from the long bus rides. Once I got off the bus, an older guy approached me as I walked towards the mall.

"Hey beautiful, do you mind if I get your number?" Looking back, a white man who was old enough to be my father, was standing by an all-black Lincoln. I immediately felt sick to my stomach, a feeling I always felt from being taken advantage of by older men. I held my composure and walked over to him. "I don't give my number out, but I can take yours."

"Well, as long as you're going to use it, I don't mind giving it to you." He flashed a perfect smile, with a set of beautiful pearly white teeth before handing me a business card. Looking over his entire body, I tried to see if there was anything I recognized, but there wasn't anything that triggered my memory. He was handsome to be an older guy, he had a light scar that was slightly visible on the side of his face. His scent was recognizable also, he wore Nautica. I grew to hate that damn smell, I was able to name cologne fragrance, due to all the men who raped me. To keep my mind off of what they were doing, I would find something else to focus on. "You okay there beautiful?" The man said, snapping me out of my trance. "Yeah, I'm fine," I told him while brushing my feelings off.

"I don't think I introduced myself properly, my name is Kevin. I own a car lot by the Pork and Beans project, come check me out sometime." "How long have you owned that?" I asked him without any hesitation. "I'd say, for over 20 years. Business is great," he boasted.

That was all the information I needed; as dollar signs flashed before my eyes "I'm going to let you go, but I hope to hear from you."

"Oh, don't worry, you will." I told him, while giving him an innocent but sexy smile. I left him standing there, hoping he would get a good look at my fat ass. I knew I had him when I looked back and saw him still watching me as I walked away.

Spending almost the entire day shopping, eased my mind some. I had about $5,000 on me and I was treating myself like a queen. I wanted to get my hair done but I would miss the bus, so I decided against it at the last minute. Instead I purchased a coloring kit and a cell phone, then headed for the bus stop.

Riding the bus took forever, I was drained physically. It felt good being able to buy nice things, being 15 and alone didn't seem too bad after all.

I had a hard time trying to figure out how to work my new phone, I was so lost with the latest technology. Once the bus came to a stop, I gathered all of my bags and got off. The bus stop was about 2 blocks from the motel. It was a little after 10 pm, so I hurriedly walked down the dark street. "Let me help you with that sexy mama." A tall guy called out, he was walking on the opposite side of the street with about three others guys. I ignored him and continued to walk towards my room. Finally, I made it to my room, but I was scared to open up the door. The group of men followed close behind me, even with a razor in my mouth, I was still outnumbered and wouldn't be able to take all 4 of them. "I said let me help you, can't a nigga be nice?" The tall dude said, as he walked closer to me. "I'm fine, but thank you." I tried to be as polite as I could, while trying to avoid any bruised egos. Before I could attempt to unlock my room door, the tall guy placed a gun to my back while the other one snatched my keys. They opened my room door and forced me inside. I had a feeling this wouldn't end too well. "Next time someone offers to help you, take the help bitch." I wanted to put up a fight, but with a gun pointed at me, there wasn't much I could do. Something told me to grab the gun before I left, now here I was in another fucked up predicament. I didn't want to carry a gun through the mall, so I decided to leave it, now I was regretting it. I spit my razor into my hand, hoping I could take one of their asses out before they took me out. "Yo, Dom. Make that bitch strip," one of the dudes, told the tall guy. At that point, visions of me being 5 years old again played in my head. "Don't say my fucking name Alex, the tall guy yelled back at his companion." They were both arguing, as the other two just looked at me lustfully. With the razor in my hand, I jumped up and swung, almost cutting Alex on the side of his face. Before I could connect, all four of them jumped on me, their fist connected with every part of my body. I curled up in a ball, but that didn't stop them from beating my ass. "Wait, I'm only 15, I yelled." They stopped hitting me, but Dom smiled mischievously. "That means the pussy is fresh, let's get it boys," Dom ordered. My clothes were being ripped off in every which direction; my cries only fueled them even more. For over 3 hours, all four of them took turns raping me. I was going in and out of consciousness, as they tore my vagina and ripped me a new asshole. Before I passed out, I took a good look at each and every one of them. I would remember features, smells and anything else that would help me identify them if I made it out of here alive. Even with one of my eyes swollen shut, I didn't let it stop me from taking mental notes. Alex wrapped his shirt around my neck, they were torturing me profoundly. Dom was behind me, ramming himself in my ass, while one of his boys rammed his dick down my throat. Alex stood off to the side, holding his shirt tightly around my neck making sure I didn't move, as the fourth guy was recording and jerking his tiny penis. With the last bit of dignity I did have, I bit down on the dude's dick as hard as I could. He screamed in agony at the top of his lungs, "This bitch is biting me." Tears ran down his face, as he tried to fight the pain. Alex then pulled the shirt tighter around my neck, blood formed in my mouth, from biting the guy's dick halfway off. I spit the blood out in Dom's face, he punched me hard as fuck and his fist landed right by my temple. That hit took me out, I collapsed right on the bed in a daze. Whatever else they did to me after that, I wouldn't be able to speak on. I got knocked out like an amature boxer, but this time I didn't go out without a fight.

CHAPTER 7
Left for Dead

Waking up bloody and bruised, I felt completely numb. My body felt weak and the pain was excruciating. I had a knot the size of a golf ball, on the side of my head. One of my eyes was closed shut and my vagina felt like it was on fire, blood was everywhere.

"Knock knock"

A light tap at the door startled me, unable to move or speak. I laid on the bed motionless. I was silently praying that the guys who raped and tortured me weren't coming back.

An older lady yelled out,

"Housekeeping". In a spanish accent.

A bit relieved, I continued to lay there. The door clicked, as the housekeeper entered the room.

"Oh Dios mío(Oh my God), somebody help." She yelled frantically in spanish. Another unknown person ran to my room, they looked at me and immediately called the cops.

Moments later, two officers arrived followed by an ambulance. I was placed on a stretcher, and hauled off to the emergency room. The amount of pain I felt was unendurable. My right eye was still swollen shut, my ribs ached, my leg felt like it was broken and I reeked of urine from pissing on myself. As soon as we arrived, I was admitted and left in a cold room all alone.

Hours went by, before I was greeted by a female doctor. "Hello there Mrs. Boykins," the doctor addressed me by the fake name I provided. I didn't respond so she continued, "I know you're in lots of pain, so we gave you some medication in your I.V. you should feel some relief momentarily, we have also performed a rape kit on you. Unfortunately, I have bad news for you." She looked down at the floor briefly before she continued to speak, so I knew whatever was next, wouldn't be anything good. "You've tested positive for herpes, as well as chlamydia. No signs of HIV have been detected as of yet, but it's important you have a follow up appointment just to be safe." "I'm so sorry, but I want you to know, we have counselors who can assist you further." I couldn't even cry anymore, I had nothing left in me. All my life, all folks did was take from me. I could feel the medication kicking in, so I closed my eyes and fell into a deep sleep.

8 months later, I was released from the hospital. After I fell asleep, I didn't wake back up. I was placed in a medically induced coma, after the doctors realized I had bleeding on my brain. After a successful surgery, they were able to get the hemorrhaging on my brain under control. I was told several times; I was lucky to be alive. It didn't dawn on me until today, that I missed my sweet 16th. I guess it didn't matter anyhow, I didn't have anyone to celebrate with me. Looking at the calendar, I felt so confused as almost an entire year went by. I didn't look the same at all, I was really thin. My body looked completely different; I was no longer thick and flawless, instead I was frail with a sunken face and dry skin. Prior to my release, they gave me medication to clear up the chlamydia, the herpes would be something I'd have to live with since there was no cure. They gave me some information on both diseases, but I refused counseling. Who

the fuck was gone talk to me when they had no idea of all the shit I've been through? There was no helping me now, when I needed help I had none. I picked up my phone, trying to remember if I had anyone who could give me a ride home. I only had a few contacts, I was dumbfounded when I came across a man named Kevin. Instead of calling just anyone I opt for an uber.

Once I got back to the motel, the lady who found me greeted me. "Hola hermosa." "I'm so happy you're okay darling, we saved your room since you paid for the year." Her heavy spanish accent gave me flashbacks.

I gave her a light hug and thanked her for saving my life, I made my way inside my room and instantly became sick. Everywhere I looked, memories of the attack flashed before me. "Do you think I can switch rooms?" I asked the housekeeper." "Yes of course, I'll put you on the other side," she said politely, I started gathering my belongings to head over to my new room, I just remembered that I left all the money here. I dropped to my knees and looked under the bed, the backpack was gone. I ran to the dresser, the jewelry was there and the gun was in the same spot. The weed was also still there. I couldn't believe all my money was fucking gone; I was back at square one. The only good thing was, my room was paid for a few more months. I still had the Jewelry, so I'd go see how much I could get for it. I had about $1,500 left in my pocket, I would have been fucked, if the assholes who raped me ran my pockets too.

"Your room is ready hermosa."

The housekeeper startled me, as she poked her head in my room. "Thank you again, I appreciate all of your help."

She helped me take all of my belongings to the other room, I gave her a $10 tip for her help. I didn't want to give her that, but she was a nice older lady. Once I got everything situated, I grabbed a pen and my notepad and made my way into the bathroom. I ran a nice hot bath and used some body wash to make some bubbles. Sitting in the tub, I began to write in my notepad. I added Alex and Dom, since I knew them by name. The other two who raped me, I added everything I could remember about them. The shorter dude had cornrows, dark brown eyes, with a scar on his cheek and he smelled like weed, he was the camera man. The other guy was heavy set, he wore a low fade, I was certain he was Puerto Rican, his dick was the one that I almost bit off. One thing about me was, I'd never forget a face. Even after being in the hospital, and undergoing surgery, I still had some of the details fresh in my memory. They may have thought they got away with hurting me, but I was going to catch them one by one.

After I stepped out of the tub, I threw on a nightgown. I grabbed my dye, as well as the other products I bought. This would be my first time ever doing anything to my hair, let alone cutting it. I was going to cut my hair length, from my butt to a bob. Once that was completed, I'd dye it blonde. I grabbed my phone, and watched a youtube tutorial, on how to properly do a hair makeover. After watching the video over and over, I attempted to start my makeover.

Looking in the mirror, I stared at my reflection. My hair was cut shoulder length, styled into a bob. I wore green contacts, and my hair was bright blonde. I thought the blonde was a little too bright, but it would have to do for now. I added makeup over my eyes and put dark burgundy lipstick on. I lost about 40 pounds from being in the hospital, I went from a size 16 to a size 8. I was so happy I bought dresses, and one size fits all items, otherwise my entire wardrobe would be pointless. I guess the weight loss would help with my new appearance as well, I didn't like it but I had to use it to my advantage.

I was getting ready to go to the pharmacy, this would be my first time out since the incident. Hopefully I wouldnt come across any trouble, since the pharmacy was about two blocks away.

Before leaving the motel, I put my razor in my mouth. Something told me to grab the gun, so I placed it into my belt loop. I refused to be a victim again, this time I'd shoot a mothafucka before they hurt me.

Once I got to the pharmacy, the lady behind the counter said it would only be a few minutes to fill my prescription, so I sat and waited.

"Ma'am I'll need to see your I.D. as well as your insurance card, in order for me to give you your medication." The pharmacist said, while waiting for me to hand her my information. "I don't have any information on me, my wallet was stolen. I was raped and beat, as well as robbed," I told her, while crying dramatically. "Ok, calm down sweetie." She tried to hush me, so I wouldn't cause a scene in front of the other customers. She advised me to sign some paperwork, which I did. "Next time, I won't be able to do this. I could lose my job, so make sure you have proper identification next time," she informed me. I nodded my head, and made my way out of the store.

As I started to walk down Jefferson street, I put my hoodie up and made my way back to the motel. About 2 feet in front of me I heard two familiar voices. Trying to be as unnoticeable as possible, I stood by a bus stop and put my head down.

"Alright Alex, hit my line tomorrow." The voice I recognized was Dom's. Giving each other a pound, Dom walked across the street, making his way into a brick house. Alex continued to walk up the block alone. I started walking again, making sure to keep my distance. After walking two more blocks, I shortened the distance between us. "Aye, you got some work," I called out to Alex. He turned around, looking at me suspiciously. "Nah, I ain't got nothing for you" he replied. Well I got something for you I said, while taking off my hood. "You don't recognize me Mr. Choker?" "Don't you like to choke bitches with your shirt?" His eyes widened, as he finally realized who I was. "You stupid bitch, you killed my cousin. Because of that stupid ass stunt you pulled, he lost so much blood that he went into cardiac arrest. Now he's gone, cause you want to bite niggas dick's off you fucking psycho."

I couldn't believe he was blaming me for what I did, when they were the ones who raped me, I thought to myself. "Well, now you can join him," I pulled out the gun, holding it steadily like I learned from youtube. He looked at me confused, like he wanted to either try me or run. I pointed the gun directly at his face, I pulled the trigger but nothing happened. Alex took a deep breath before he turned around and ran. Looking over the gun, I took the safety off.

"Pop! Pop! Pop!

I fired the gun three times, the force almost made me lose my balance. Alex's body thumped to the ground, as he screamed out in pain. I made my way over to him, he was squirming around like a fish out of water. "Who's the stupid bitch now?" I spat, while Pulling the trigger once again. I put a bullet right in the middle of his forehead, it didn't even phase me when I did it and that scared me a little bit. I tucked the gun and put my hoodie back up.

Once I made it back to my room, I jumped right in the shower. My hands were shaking and I had blood on my shirt. I scrubbed my body for about an hour, before getting out. I never shot anyone before, maybe sliced a few people but that was it. I had to get used to this shit, I had a lot more people who needed to disappear. Grabbing my pen and notepad, I crossed out Alex's name. I was assuming his cousin was the heavy-set dude, Alex was Rican and so was he. I crossed out all the details about the heavy-set dude, since he was already dead. I wonder what they said happened to him, I'm sure they didn't say he was raping someone and got his dick bitten off. It put me at ease, knowing two of them were gone. After updating my notepad, I rolled a fat blunt. I had to do something to take my mind off of this shit, getting high was the only way to escape reality temporarily. A bunch of sick fucks took advantage of me and left me for dead, now it was my turn to do the killing.

CHAPTER 8
I see you

Smoking weed was becoming a habit, I woke up hungry as hell with the munchies from smoking all night. That dead man's weed was definitely some good shit, I knew the difference between gas and trash.

There was finally some news coverage on Max, his remains were found inside but there was not much more they could say at this time. The news reporter said they had no suspects and that an update would be given when more information became available. I was satisfied knowing they had nothing, when you burn a whole damn house down there was less evidence to go on. My stomach started to growl, with nothing to eat I had to get up and make a store run for some food. Trying to maintain the little bit of cash I had, I didn't want to spend too much on junk food. A corner store was about three blocks away, so I hopped in the shower and got dressed. My new appearance was looking good on me, the knot on my head went away but underneath my eyes were still a little black and blue. I grabbed my Louis Vuitton shades that I purchased from the mall, I placed my razor in my mouth and headed out.

Walking down East Blvd, a few cars blew at me hoping to get my attention. I ignored them at first. Then I thought about how they could actually come in handy, so I put a little sexy in my walk. It wasn't long before a few cars stopped, the first guy rolled up in a beat-up Honda. "What's up blondie, how are you doing?" He asked, with a huge smile on his face. I'm good, but I'm taken. I replied harshly. "Well fuck you." He yelled, as he sped off. I didn't have time for some low-class wannabe, I needed a nigga with bread. No sooner then he sped off, an all-black Lincoln pulled up. "Can I give you a lift," the man asked politely. "Do I know you?" I replied back flirtatiously. "You look familiar, but I don't think we have had the pleasure of introducing ourselves. If you want, we could get to know each other ." I smiled, knowing I hit the jackpot. "How about you give me your number, after I go shopping and get dressed I'll call you." He handed me a business card, for some reason it looked familiar. "I'll call you in an hour," I told him as I walked away. Kevin was the name on his business card, I went to my contacts in my phone to see if this was the same number. The exact same number was already programmed in my phone, I guess the coma did have an effect on some of my memory, I forgot where I knew him from. I didn't like this at all, all I had on my side was memories of people. However, he didn't recognize me either, so whatever happened between us couldn't have been too serious. I'm Heavenly for a reason, I leave a long lasting impression on people, I'm not easy to forget. I pushed my egotistical thoughts away and continued to make my way to the store.

Once inside, I purchased enough items to put in my mini fridge as well as some snacks. I paid for the items and walked back to my room. One block away from the motel, I saw Dom walking towards me with a short chick. I was mad as hell I was carrying all this shit, I wanted to kill that nigga right there. I slowed down a bit, hoping we would walk past each other. Once they were close enough, I was able to see the girls face. Dom was walking with Kacey, now that was a surprise. I would have never expected to see Kacey, especially not on this side of town. Now that I knew she was involved with Dom; I would use that to my advantage. Kacey never really did anything to me, she was just guilty by association.

"Damn Dom, you see something you like?" I overheard Kacey talking to Dom as I walked by, he glanced my way briefly. I looked at him, and mouthed "I see you," while winking at him. "Nah baby, I thought I knew her" he lied. They both made their way down the street, towards the house I saw him go into the other night.

I made it back to my room with a plan for Dom, I opened my drawer to grab my medicine. I was hoping the medication was working, so I wouldn't have any outbreaks. Having herpes, I knew that an outbreak could occur at any given moment. I freshened up, and picked out a black dress, with thigh high boots. I wanted to look sexy for Kevin, so that he could give me whatever my heart desired. After getting dressed, I fixed my hair up. I was still rocking my bob, and my green contacts were still in. A little nervous, I finally placed a call to Kevin.

Picking up on the first ring, his voice was extremely low. "Hello," he answered. "Hey Kevin, it's Rayne."

"Give me just one minute," he whispered. After a few minutes of hearing him moving around, his entire demeanor changed when he got back on the phone. "Well I'm assuming you're the beauty I saw walking earlier; I have been waiting for you to call." I can't front, this old ass man had me blushing. "Are you busy right now?" I asked, giving a hint that I wanted him to come get me. "Not at all, would you like to have some dinner?"

"I'd love to," I told him. After giving him the location for pick up, we ended the call. All I really wanted was to get in good with him, hopefully he would eventually give me a car. I needed my own transportation, walking these streets alone, or catching busses was not for me.

About an hour passed by, before my phone went off. Kevin texted me, letting me no he was outside. I didn't give him my room number, but I did tell him I was staying at a motel. Once he saw me coming, he got out of the car and opened the door for me. "Thank you," I said while planting a kiss on his cheek and making my way inside of his car.

"So, where did you get the name Rayne from? That is very unique," Kevin asked. "I was born on a wet and rainy day, so my mother decided to name me that." "Wow, that's interesting." We both laughed.

"So, Rayne, how old are you?" My dumbass almost told him my real age, with quick thinking I blurted out that I was 19. "I'm quite older than you, but age is just a number, right?" Kevin said it like he was telling me, instead of asking me. "Of course it is," I assured him. "Listen Kevin, before you go any further, I really don't like to get too deep into my personal life. I'm a loner and I have absolutely no one and no family." "Really? I wouldn't expect such a beautiful girl, such as yourself to be all alone."

"Well now you know" I mumbled.

"As long as you take care of me, I'll take care of you." Kevin said, while grabbing my hand.

We arrived at a restaurant, but I wasn't familiar with it at all. I smiled a little when I saw the name of the restaurant, it was called Crazy About You. From the outside, you could tell it was expensive. I felt like I wasn't dressed appropriately, but Kevin reassured me that I looked beautiful. He was the perfect gentleman, he wore a black Gucci two-piece suit, with black Gucci dress shoes. He sported a fresh crew cut, with a diamond earring in his ear. Kevin really had soul, he gave me the Brad Pitt type of vibe, just the hood version.

To my surprise, Kevin had already made reservations. So, we were seated promptly, without waiting in the long lines. Once we were seated, Kevin ordered us some Chardonnay. "May I see your identification," the waiter asked me. Kevin looked at me, sensing my hesitation, he took control of the situation. "Hey Austin, cut her some slack, she's with me man." Obviously, Kevin was a regular, he knew mostly everyone here by name. The waiter nodded his head and went to grab our bottle. "Do you have any identification Rayne?" "I'm going to take you around the world and it will require your ID." "To be honest Kevin, I don't. I have nothing, I was thrown in a group home at a young age, I ran away and since then, I've just been running." "I'm sorry to hear that, I have a few friends who can help us out.

Tomorrow, I'll get you everything you need," he promised. "I can't thank you enough, you've been good to me, but you don't even know me and my name is spelled R-A-Y-N-E."

"I see so much potential in you Rayne, you remind me so much of".... Kevin stopped what he was saying, then continued. "Let me just say this, I like you already." I didn't respond, I just smiled. The waiter interrupted our conversation, as he placed a bucket of ice and our bottle of wine on the table. "Are you ready to order," the waiter asked. I gave him my order; I chose the Surf and Turf Kobe Mini-Burgers. Kevin ordered the Hawaiian Tuna Poke salad.

Dinner was great, the food was delicious. It's been awhile since I had a nice dinner. Kevin and I left the restaurant hand and hand, I hated for the night to end. Once we got back to the motel, we sat and talked in his car. Out of the corner of my eye, I saw Dom walking past and immediately cut the conversation short. "Thank you for tonight Kevin, I appreciate you." Kevin kissed my forehead, "The pleasure was all mine." "I apologize if you feel like I'm cutting you short, but I should get going." I said my goodbyes to Kevin and made my way towards my room. Once Kevin pulled off I started running to my room, I grabbed my razor and placed it in my mouth. Dom couldn't have got too far I thought, so I walked down the block. One block over, he was standing on the corner. "Where are you going sexy," he shouted from across the street. "I'm going to the store; I'll be right back." I went into the local convenience store and purchased a few items. The items consist of a cucumber, sleeping pills, bleach, and cooking oil. I made my way back down the block, Dom was still standing at the corner. "Do you mind if I join you tonight?" he asked while walking beside me. "I don't mind at all, I could use some company."

"I saw you the other day with a girl, was that your girlfriend?"

"Nah, she was just a jealous friend." He lied. We made it back to the motel, there was a spare room that was always unlocked, so I took him into that room. It was about three doors down from the room I stayed in. I poured us both a drink, making sure I made his a little special by adding lots of powder from the pills. Handing him his drink, I sat down on the bed with him. "Do you smoke?" I asked.

"Yeah, what you got?"

I grabbed some weed out my purse and rolled a blunt, we smoked two blunts back to back. A few minutes later, Dom laid down on the bed. "Damn, that was some gas, shit got me tired." I looked over at Dom, it was evident that the powder from the pills that I put in his drink were working. Dom was trying to fight the urge to sleep, the combination of the drugs and pills finally took over.

Grabbing two bed sheets from the dresser, I tied his hands up and covered his mouth with tape. Grabbing the cucumber from the bag, I pulled his pants down. He laid on his stomach, butt ass naked. Excitement took over me, as I attempted to ram the cucumber up his ass. Dom woke up confused, but he couldn't move. Struggling to release himself, he made several attempts to untie his hands. I poured the oil on the cucumber. "You like to rape people, right? You like ramming your nasty ass dick in people's ass. Now look at your stupid ass, tied the fuck up by the person you raped. Now I'm going to rape you, with this fat ass cucumber. I want to see how you feel, after I'm done with you, you can join Alex in hell." Dom tried hard to untie his hands, but of course he was unsuccessful. With the cucumber dripping with oil, I climbed on the bed so I could position myself properly. I rammed the cucumber up his ass forcefully, I did it repeatedly until my hands got tired. I started laughing hysterically when I saw his asshole bleeding. "How does it feel Dom?" He laid motionless on the bed, tormented by the pain I was causing him. Jumping off the bed, I walked to the right side of him. I grabbed a hold of his hair, pulling his head all the way back. It was obvious that he was in pain, little did he know it wasn't over yet. "Would you like to say anything?" I asked him, while taking the tape off his mouth. "Fuck you," he whispered. I smiled at him, before spitting my razor out my mouth. "Nah, fuck you."

"I told you, I would see you again. A part of me really wanted him to say he was sorry, I wanted him to beg for his life. A little disappointed, I placed the tape back over his mouth. Holding him by his hair tightly, I slit his throat. I untied him, and took the tape off his mouth. Blood poured from his mouth and his nose, I stood there until he stopped fighting and took his last breath. Cleaning the entire room with bleach, I made sure to wipe everything down. Gathering everything I came with, I made sure to check over the room a few more times. I flushed the razor down the toilet and left out the room quickly. Killing Dom felt good, but torturing him made me feel powerful. As soon as I got back to my room I headed straight to the shower, Dom's blood was still under my nails. I could see this killing shit was about to become the norm for me. Instead of crying about who I was becoming, I let my fingers take control and I busted a killer nut.

CHAPTER 9
Fake Friends

"Police, open up!" Two days passed since the incident with Dom. I've been ignoring Kevin's call's, I haven't eaten and I've been in bed since. Now I was being awakened by pounding at the door, police commands being shouted loudly from the hall. Getting out of my bed, I opened the door. "Good afternoon ma'am, my name is detective O'Rielly." "We are conducting an investigation for a possible homicide."

"A homicide?" I asked, looking at the detective in disbelief. The detective continued speaking. "Yes ma'am, a few doors down. I've been going door to door inquiring about anything suspicious, or out of the ordinary the last few days?"

"No sir, I have been really sick. I've actually been bed ridden the last couple of days. I'm sorry I can't be of any help, this is very awful." I spoke quietly, while doing a few dramatic coughs. "Thank you for your time, if you hear anything please contact me." The detective handed me his card and walked away.

My heart started beating fast, I sat down on the bed. Thinking back to the night I killed Dom, I replayed back everything in my head. I was hoping and praying I didn't leave anything that would lead back to me, I knew I bleached everything down, but what if I left some kind of DNA behind. Taking a deep breath, I tried not to panic. I could hear people talking outside so I fixed my hair and make-up, I slipped from my room and joined the crowd. As soon as I stepped outside, Kacey was the first person I noticed. She was crying hysterically, while talking to a cop. "He was my boyfriend, I loved him so much." Kacey cried. I took that as my que, to go over and try to console her. In my head, I really wanted to slice her fucking throat.

Approaching Kacey, I placed my hand on her shoulder. "I'm so sorry for your loss, I know how you're feeling right now, I lost my boyfriend just two weeks ago," I lied. "Really? So, you know the pain I feel then?" I wanted to gag, as snot dripped from her nose. She turned to face me, looking at me for a short period of time. "You look familiar, do we know each other?" She asked. I hope she wouldn't recognize me, otherwise I'd be fucked. I saw you and your boyfriend walking a few times, but I'm new to the area.

"Well, my name is Kacey." She reached her hand out, I observed it for snot and buggers before reluctantly shaking it. "My name is Rayne, it's nice to meet you. If you would like, we can go to my room and talk. The least I can do, is offer you some emotional support." "When my boyfriend died, I didn't have anyone to talk to."

"I'm sorry to hear that girl, it would be my pleasure to take you up on your offer." The crowd slowly dispersed, as the body of Dom was removed from the motel. Kacey cried out loudly, as she witnessed Dom being taken away. Grabbing her hand, I led her to my room. "Make yourself at home, I'm going to roll a blunt, do you smoke?"

"Yes, I sure do. Anything to take my mind off this shit, I still can't believe he's gone. The crazy thing is, his best friend was shot and killed last week" Kacey said, as she began to get emotional again. "I didn't want to hear this bitch whining all day, so I rolled a fat ass L, hoping she would shut the fuck up. I was good at being a fake ass friend, I needed to get close to her, so she could lead me to Saharra and Chaz. Hearing about Dom and his friend, was not something I wanted to hear right now. Hell, I'm the one who killed the mothafuckas," I thought.

My phone started buzzing, I picked it up off the dresser. Kevin was calling for the 20th time. "Hello," I answered, barely above a whisper. "So now you finally decided to pick up, what's going on Rayne?" You could tell Kevin was aggravated with me, just by the tone of his voice. "I've been sick for the past two days; I haven't been able to move or eat. Not only that, but someone was murdered a few doors down from me."

"Damn Rayne, all you had to do was pick up, I could have taken care of you. I think it's best we get you out of that area, it doesn't seem to be the safest place." A smile crossed my face, it seemed like Kevin genuinely cared for me. "I really don't like taking things from people, I'm more of a get it how I can type of girl." I was saying everything I knew he wanted to hear.

"Listen here Rayne, I'll be over to drop off something to you, so make sure you answer," Kevin said before we ended our call.

"Did you get over your boyfriend already?" Kacey asked sarcastically. "Nah, I didn't. I also think you should mind your business, that was my uncle Kevin."

"My bad girl, calm down. I really wasn't trying to be funny, I just wanted to see how long it would take for me to get over Dom." She said, apologetically. "Everyone heals differently, so no one can tell you how long."

"Without Dom, I have no one. I feel so hopeless, now I'm homeless." Kacey began to vent again, but this time I wanted to get more out of her, so I went with the flow. "How old are you Kacey?"

"I'm 16" she replied. "Wow, your young. I'm 19, but I've lived life, like I'm 30" I laughed. "At 20, you would think I'm living my best life. Truth is, I have no friends, no family and this motel has been my home. My uncle just came into my life, only a few months ago."

"Damn, that's crazy Kacey said. "I guess we are in the same boat, the only difference is, I have a few friends. My best friend is Saharra, but she is usually tied up with her no-good ass boyfriend. My parents disowned me, after I dropped out of high school. They said if I didn't care about my future neither would they. I left home and started talking to Dom, which distracted me from school even more. He hung out with three other people. I looked at them like older brother's, since they all were about seven years older than me." My stomach churned, just thinking about Dom and his friends. He was way too old, to be talking to a 16-year-old girl. It made me even happier, that I killed his perverted ass, I thought to myself. I didn't interrupt her at all, I wanted her to keep talking. "Now since Dom is gone, I have no one." I've been staying with him for the past year."

"Why don't you stay with your best friend?" I dug a little further.

"Her parents won't allow me too." Kacey said sadly. "She was attacked at school, a little while ago. A girl named Heavenly sliced her up pretty bad."

"Damn, that's crazy," I mumbled.

"Why did you say her boyfriend was no good?" I asked, trying not to seem too interested. "He's the reason why Saharra was attacked, he would always flirt with girls, Heavenly just happened to be someone Saharra despised."

"So basically, Saharra is a bully, her boyfriend is a coward, and you were just the follower?" Kacey looked at me before answering that question. "I guess you can say that, but I never did anything to Heavenly, she was just a sad girl. She was always dressed poorly and she didn't have any friends." Damn, that sounds just like me, I laughed almost too loud. "Your beautiful tho, I'm not saying Heavenly wasn't pretty, but you're bad. "I knew I was wrong for not intervening, especially when Saharra would pick with her. But Saharra was popular in school, I wanted to be popular too. I had no other friends, besides Saharra. When I moved to Miami, she was the only person who wanted to be my friend. It's sad to say, I was like Heavenly but Saharra saved me."

"Are you and Sarah still close?" I asked, quickly changing the subject. "Her name is Saharra and yes, we are still friends." The problem is, she lives in Bal Harbour, no buses go that way."

We ended our conversation for now, as we continued to puff and pass. I wanted to stop her from rambling too much, she sure did spill the beans.

I kind of felt Kacey had good intentions, she didn't know how to stand up for herself let alone somebody else. She was a very pretty brown skin girl, with shoulder length curly black hair and brown eyes. She was thin and had dimples in her cheeks. Everytime she smiled, her deep dimples made her a little more attractive. We could have possibly been very good friends, if only the circumstances were different.

After gathering all that information from Kacey, I thought it was best to keep her around. Before I could ask her anything, my phone went off.

"I'm outside," Kevin said when I answered. I made my way out to the parking lot, leaving Kacey in the room. Kevin was standing outside of his car. "Hello beautiful, I'm glad you're feeling better." "Thank you, I'm not one hundred percent yet, but I'll be fine." Kevin gave me a light kiss on the cheek, before handing me an envelope. "I don't want you to open it now, wait until you go back inside," he instructed. "Give me a call later, let me know what you think." Kevin got back in his car, he winked at me before pulling off.

Once I got back to the room, Kacey nosy ass wanted to know why he showed up. I went straight to the bathroom ignoring her completely, when I opened up the envelope, my mouth dropped. Somehow, Kevin was able to get me an ID. A picture of a girl who looked almost like me was on it, with Ryane Shine as my name. There was also a stack of money, attached to it was a note. I began to read it. *"Rayne, you came into my life and blew me away. I want nothing more, than for you to get out of that place you're in. Here is some money, so that you can furnish your new apartment."* Taped to the side of the envelope was a key, the address was written at the bottom of the letter. Tears formed in my eyes, but I refused to let them fall. "Are you okay in there," Kacey asked from outside the bathroom door. "Yes, I'll be out in a minute." Counting the money inside the envelope, there was $10,000 inside. I stepped out of the bathroom, with a huge smile on my face. "What's up girl, everything alright?"

"Everything is just fine, my family will always look out for me." I flashed the wad of bills Kevin gave me. Kacey just looked at me, I guess she didn't know how to react. "Listen Kacey, how about you freshen up, so you can show me around the neighborhood. I'll take you shopping and we both can grab a few things."

"I think that would be great Rayne, thank you for being so supportive. I never had anyone do anything good for me, so please don't think I'm trying to rain on your parade." Kacey gave me a hug, while making her way to the shower. I didn't know how I would make Kacey suffer, or if I would. I was kind of confused for once; I didn't know if I wanted to be a fake friend, or a real enemy.

CHAPTER 10
My Enemy My Friend

"**H**appy Birthday Rayne." Kevin woke me up, holding roses in his hand. Today was my 18th birthday, but according to my I.D. It was my 21st Birthday. I was telling Kevin so many lies, I had to make sure I could keep up with them. Over the last two years, Kevin has been nothing but good to me. I had a condo to call my own, since he purchased it for me and told me to never step foot in a motel again. I was so grateful, but all I could offer in return was some young wet pussy. "Hey honey, I have a surprise for you, so get yourself together." Kevin had so much excitement in his voice, I knew whatever the surprise was it would be worth it. Last year he gave me a matching diamond set, I wasn't into jewelry too much; however the necklace and earrings were beautiful, but they would never replace my necklace Zoe bought me for my 5th birthday.

Getting up, I went straight for the bathroom. I had to brush my teeth and freshen up. Kevin's house was beautiful, he had 6-bedrooms and 4 bathrooms in his mini mansion. He made sure I kept a toothbrush, as well as a change of clothing here. Even though he purchased me a condo, this was also like my home. Kevin was an old freak, he liked being whipped and spanked during sex. When we first fucked, I was so uncomfortable with his demands. Putting my finger in his ass, or telling him to lick my shoe, is some of the things he desired. I started making myself get used to it, because he would pay me lovely.

"Rayne, c'mon. I've been waiting for you; I have to go to the shop in 20 minutes." Kevin was yelling from downstairs, rushing me as usual. Once I made my way downstairs, there was a box on the last step. I bent down to pick it up, inside was $5,000. Smiling, I continued to walk towards the front of the house. "I'm out here." Kevin said quickly. I was able to determine he was out in the garage, even with his quick response. Once I opened the door that led to the garage, my mouth damn near hit the floor. Parked in the driveway, was a pink Porsche, with a huge pink bow on the hood. "Don't just look at it, hop in and take it for a spin. I haven't been teaching you how to drive, for the past year for nothing." Kevin said, as he held open the door for me. I wanted to call Kacey so bad, but Kevin didn't know I was dealing with her. The only reason I kept Kacey a secret, is because she was my trick partner. Yes, I said trick partner. I got caught up in the lavish lifestyle and didn't want to ask Kevin for money all the time. Any time I wanted money from him, he would want me to perform weird sex acts. One time, I had to tie him up and spank him with a broom. Another time, he wanted me to finger him while sucking his dick. Don't get me wrong I loved money, but sometimes I just wanted quick money. That's how I got into tricking, since last year I have been turning tricks with Kacey. Kevin thought I had an actual job; in all actuality I was fucking for money. He was too busy running the shop, to worry about what I was doing. Hopping in my new car, I headed right to the motel, we kept the same room for over 2 years. I'd surprise Kacey, and take her for a spin since she usually sat in the room anyway.

Once I made it to the motel, I called Kacey, but she didn't answer. I got out of my car and made my way to our room. Even though I had my own spot, I still helped pay for this room for our business. know one knows where I lay my head at and I wanted to keep it like that. I used my key to open the door, to my surprise Kacey was sitting with Chaz and Saharra. I haven't seen these two since the incident at school years ago, I held my composure. "Hey Rayne, this is my best friend and her boyfriend I'm always talking to you about." I gave them a dry, "hello." I was in a good mood, I wasn't going to let my enemies of my friend ruin my day. Looking at Saharra only fueled bad memories. I gave Chaz a glance, he didn't even look the same. It looked like they both were going through hell, but it just wasn't the hell I wanted them to face. Saharra wasn't the pretty slim girl anymore, she looked like she gained about 60 pounds, Chaz looked like he gained about 40 pounds. Chaz was trying to get my attention, when I looked at him he smiled. I just ignored him, as visions back in high school played in my head. "Well Kacey, let me know when you're done, Kevin bought me a new whip and I wanted to take you for a ride."

"A new car? Damn Rayne, I want to see it." Kacey slid on her flip flops and motioned for Saharra and Chaz to follow. "Oh shit bitch, this is fucking fly." Kacey said, as we all walked towards my car. "Nice car, you should take us all for a ride." Saharra replied. "Girl, I don't even know you, my friend, friends aren't my friends," I said with much attitude. "Rayne is not a people person, don't pay her no mind." Kacey interjected, while trying to ease the tension. Saharra rolled her eyes, making her way back to the room. Saharra may not recognize me, but I could never forget her ass. Even if Kacey didn't introduce us, her face would always be one I'd remember.

"Hey beautiful, why don't you take my number?" Chaz said, snapping me out of my thoughts. He was standing by my car smoking a cigarette, I was that zoned out I didn't realize he was standing there alone. "It would be my pleasure," I told him, while slipping his number in my pocket. "That blonde fits you, your green eyes make you look so sophisticated," Chaz complimented me. "Thank you," I replied while batting my eyes at him.

"Rayne, would you mind giving these two a ride home?" Kacey asked, while Saharra looked at Chaz like she wanted to kill him, for talking to me. I wanted to punch Kacey in her face for volunteering my services, but I had to think about it. If I gave them a ride, I'd know exactly where they lived. Instead of being a bitch, I just responded with a casual, "sure hop on it."

It took roughly a half hour to get to Saharra's house, her address was 56932 Bal Harbour place. She stayed in an high end area; it would be nearly impossible to commit a crime here. Now that I Knew where she slept, I'd make sure she'd never wake up again. I felt chills throughout my body, just thinking about sweet revenge. Even though for the last two years, Kacey has been a friend to me, her friends were my enemies and I hated them deeply. Nothing would ever come between me killing them, no matter how much I grew to like Kacey. We left Bal Harbour and headed back.

"You don't make it ring, ring, ring." Kacey blasted my radio, as Cardi B song played. Kacey was feeling herself, sitting in the passenger seat taking in the night air. "Oh shit, stop for one minute," Kacey startled me as she looked out the window. "Stop for what girl?"

"I think that's Corey, I haven't seen him since he went into S5 after Dom died. The blood felt like it was draining from my face, as I looked over and saw who Kacey was referring to. Corey was the fourth dude who raped me. I put the car in park and sat in front of a corner store. Kacey got out, as Corey was getting into a beat-up black Chevy. After a few minutes, Kacey made her way back to the car. "Sorry girl, I had to check on a good friend." "Nah, you good, how is he?" I asked. "He's alright I guess, he's pretty torn up about Dom still. Those two were more like brother's, all of his main niggas are gone, it's even crazier because, they all died one after another."

"Damn, that's sad" I lied. "Well, I have to drop you off, I'll be back in a few hours Kevin is taking me somewhere." Kacey looked at me frowning, "really Rayne?" She pouted, while rolling her eyes. "I'm sorry Kacey it slipped my mind, I'll be back though, I promise."

After dropping Kacey off, I circled back around to the corner store. Corey was still sitting in his car, it was only obvious that he was selling bags of weed. I parked my car around the corner and walked to the store, I made sure my gun was in my purse and I slipped the razor in my mouth. Of course, my open toed pink stilettos and two-piece white romper was appealing to the eyes. "Look at this sexy ass white girl," one of the guys loitering called out, as I continued to walk towards the store. "Let me get that for you," Corey said as he opened the door for me. He must have got out of his car, when he saw me walking. "Thank you," I replied while walking into the store. I picked up a few unneeded items, then went to cash out. "I got it beautiful, I can pay for this and more." Corey said, while flirting with me heavy. "You're so sweet, I can pay for my own stuff, but if you don't mind can you walk a lady back to her car?" I gave him the puppy 's eye, so he couldn't resist. "Yeah, I can do that for you. As long as I can get them digits." I ignored his last comment, picking up my items he followed me out of the store. Corey wanted to engage in small talk, while we walked around the corner. My car was two blocks up, parked on a quiet side street. I didn't want it to be seen, just in case shit didn't go as planned. "So, where is your car? Or did you just want me to walk with you?" He smiled, feeding his own ego.

"I really just wanted you to walk with me, you're really cute and you have lots of mannerism. I like your style; I wish we would have crossed paths differently."

"What's that supposed to mean?" He questioned. Ignoring him, I grabbed his hand and walked towards an alley. Once we were out of view, I grabbed his face and placed a kiss on his cheeks. Corey looked taken back, but he smiled while returning a kiss. Do you like recording people?

"What?" He asked, with a twisted look on his face. "I'm only asking because, I remember you recording me, when your friends were raping me." Corey's face twisted again; as he attempted to walk away from me. Pulling out the gun, I pointed it at him. "Don't you move, or I'll blow your fucking head off," I told him. "Listen, I made a mistake. All of my homies are dead now, so I'm just trying to live my life." Corey said, in an apologetic tone, while holding his head down. "Do you know why they are dead Corey?" He looked up at me, after realizing I already knew his name. "I'm the one who killed them dirty bastards." I laughed wickedly, hoping I was getting to him. Corey just stared at me, looking like he was contemplating his next move. He quickly flinched at me, without thinking I fired the gun. His body dropped to the ground in a sitting position, as blood poured from his chest. "Damn, you shot me." His eyes rolled, but he regained his composure. "I'm sorry, I should have never hurt you." Corey whispered, as his mouth filled with blood. "I'm sorry too," I told him. Spitting out my razor, I grabbed his hair, and slit his throat. I tucked the gun back into my purse, and made my way down the alley.

"Freeze, put your hands up now," An officer yelled out, as I faced the opposite direction. With quick thinking, I grabbed the gun. Firing off two shots down the alley, I ran as fast as these shoes would allow me. The officer yelled out commands while letting off a few rounds, one of which flew right past my head. I knew shortcuts and all kinds of shit about this alley. Instead of panicking, I slipped off my shoe's and made my way back to my car, disposing of the razor in a sewer. I was out of breath, but I made it. Placing the bag of bullshit I bought from the store on the seat, I speed off to head to the nearest river. Using a gun was never part of my plan, I should have stuck with my razor. This gun had to go, I had to be smart now. I haven't had any problems with the police and I sure as hell didn't want any.

CHAPTER 11
It Wasn't Me

Since the incident with Corey and running from the police, I made it my business to keep a low profile. I changed my appearance once again, just to make sure I'd be unnoticeable. Instead of the green contacts, I went with blue. I changed my blonde hair to black with blond highlights. With the money Kevin has been giving me, I paid a visit to Dr. Miami, two days later. My boobs went from a 32 C to a 40 D. It wouldn't be a trip to Dr. Miami, if I didn't get my ass enhanced. I walked out of there, feeling like a new person. The pain was there, but it wasn't unbearable. I knew tomorrow would be a different story, the pain is always worse the next day. The doctor told me not to move around a lot. I didn't have a problem with that, I was holding myself hostage anyhow. Kacey has been blowing me up nonstop since I haven't answered any of her calls, I really didn't know what to say to her. Should I be like, "Yeah um, I killed the last mothafucka who raped me, which happens to be a good friend of yours, which happens to be the best friend of your boyfriend who I also killed." I knew she was pissed since I never went to pick her back up, like I promised I would. I hopped in my car, putting a donut for my butt on the seat. I sat there for a moment to send a text to Kacey.

"I'm sorry boo, Kevin wouldn't let me leave." Moments later, my phone went off. **"FUCK YOU BITCH"** in all caps was Kacey's response. I didn't bother sending another message, I would just wait until she simmered down. Throwing my phone in my purse, I made my way home.

Once I got back to my condo, I laid down in bed. A part of me was still nervous, but I rolled a blunt to ease my mind. Flicking on the television, I flicked through the channels. Stopping at the news channel, a sketch of a girl was being shown. Underneath the photo read:

Wanted for Murder

I flicked through more channels, again the photo was being shown there as well. A police chief was holding a press conference, describing what happened. It wasn't until he said, **"A young white woman, roughly between** the ages of 19-25, is wanted for murder as well as attempted murder. She is responsible for killing a man in an alleyway, an officer responded to shots fired, where he saw the suspect fleeing the scene, the suspect opened fire on the officer before fleeing on foot." I burst out in laughter; I was now at ease, but kind of pissed as well. I spent all that money getting a makeover, and that sketch looked nothing like me. The drawing was only a side view, which looked like a thin white girl. I know everyone thinks I'm white but I do have color, the sketch was far from how I looked. I guess it's better safe, than sorry and money well spent. I didn't no who that was that was wanted for murder, but it wasn't me. Trying to get comfortable in my bed, I placed a pillow between my legs. Closing my eyes, I fell asleep.

"Hello beautiful." Kevin's voice awoke me, as I jumped up out of my sleep. "Ouch, what the fuck," I snapped. A sharp pain made its way from my ass to my lower back. "I'm sorry Rayne, I didn't mean to startle you," Kevin said apologetically. "Damn girl, you look great." Kevin's eyes wandered all over my body, stopping right at my breast. "Don't think about it Kevin, I'm still trying to heal. I just got this shit done yesterday, so you have to be patient," I told him. "Well, can you at least spank me, and wrap your lips around my dick?" "I'm stressed Rayne, I need some love." Kevin was basically begging me, so I put my hand out. Reaching into his pocket, he pulled out a wad of bills. I placed them in my night stand and got to work. Kevin sat on the edge of the bed, I placed a pillow on the floor so I could be somewhat comfortable. After about five minutes of ~~sucking~~ pleasing him, he asked me to stop. "Go get the toy's Rayne, I want you to beat me real good baby." Kevin said, as he kissed my cheeks. I got up off the floor and made my way into the other room, to gather the different kinds of toys he liked. I returned with cuffs, a whip, a mouth gag and a dildo. Kevin's dick was hard as a rock, he loved this kinky shit. I wasn't as excited but I knew what I had to do, so I got to it. "Get on your knees and bark bitch," I yelled all kinds of demands to him, he did exactly what I told him. Kevin got on his hands and knees, crawling towards me. "Lick my feet," I ordered, while slapping him three times with the whip. After he licked my feet, I tied the mouth gag around him, grabbed some oil off the stand and soaked the dildo. I had Kevin in all types of positions, he was turned on and it didn't take long for him to reach his happy ending. I was happy he got his nut off so quickly, I just wanted to lay down and go back to sleep.

Kevin jumped in the shower, then put on a fresh suit. He kept clothing here, just like I kept mine at his house. Looking at him, you would never know he likes his butthole played with. "Did you hear about that shooting downtown?" Kevin asked, as he fixed his tie. "I'm so glad you're out of that area, it's bad enough my business is dead smack in the middle of the bullshit. I'm thinking about relocating to ATL soon, my business is decreasing and half of my clients are afraid of the Pork and Bean projects." "Every day there's a shoot-out, I'm losing money." You could see the stress written all over Kevin's face, his eyes had bags underneath them. I ignored his question, but stood up to give him a hug. "Everything will be alright Kev, you've been in the business way too long to give up. Sometimes change is good, especially if it includes me," I told him. "You know I can't leave you, where I go you go." Kevin assured me. Staring at me briefly, he put his hands on his mouth like he was thinking about something. "Everything ok?" I asked. "Yeah, it's just every time I look at you, you remind me so much of..... Kevin stopped and walked towards the opposite side of the bedroom. "You keep saying that, but you won't tell me who I remind you of, why is that?"

"I really can't pinpoint it now, but I will eventually." Kevin kissed my neck, "I'll call you soon." He walked out the room, moments later I heard the door shut. I was kind of curious now, I wanted to know who I reminded him of. I wondered if it was an ex-girlfriend, that he didn't want to tell me about. I made my way to the shower, cleaned myself up, and went right back to sleep.

After a few weeks, my body started adjusting. I was in less pain and less tired. Kacey has been a little distant, she was still a little upset with me. But she was at least texting me now. Yesterday, she wanted to know if I heard about her friend getting killed. She said the sketch looked like a white girl, possibly a prostitute in the area. The sketch was posted all over the neighborhoods. If she didn't even notice it was supposed to be me, I knew no one would and that's what allowed me to sleep at night. I haven't seen Kacey, since my trip to Dr. Miami. I headed to the motel, to sneak up on her.

"Damn Rayne, you look good as fuck." Kacey said, while entertaining a trick. I still had the key, so I walked right in. "Thanks girl, I had to change up a little," I replied. I sat down on a chair and started rolling a blunt. Kacey was taking tricking to another level; she was fucking random dudes all day every day now. Personally, I was getting tired of it. I had about five people who I considered clients. I fucked them unprotected, but they paid me extra. I was freely passing on herpes, my chlamydia was gone but I never went back to get tested for HIV. I figured if they didn't find any then, I was good. I snapped out of my thoughts, when the guy Kacey was fucking started talking. His voice played over and over in my head, looking over at him I just knew my eyes were playing tricks on me. Biggs sat on the bed; he looked the exact same. I swear I threw up in my mouth about three times, Kacey was fucking the man who constantly raped me as a kid. I had to think shit through, I knew I could trust Kacey, but trusting her to be a witness to a murder was a bit farfetched. "Yo Kacey, hit me up later I have to make some moves right quick." I said while heading towards the door. "Damn, you're leaving already? I thought your sexy ass was joining the party," Biggs called out. "Maybe another time," I smiled and walked out. I grabbed a medal bat that someone left by their door and got in my car.

I sat inside my car, about a block away from the motel. Two hours had passed, before I finally saw Biggs leaving the room. I was even more happy that Kacey wasn't with him. It was 11:45 PM, no street lights were on. Biggs walked right past my car, then turned into an alley. I slipped my razor in my mouth and grabbed the bat. Hopping out of the car, I followed him. Once he was halfway down the alley, I sped up. Trying not to make any noise, I didn't want to alarm him until I was close enough. Lifting the bat above my head, I charged at him. He turned around slowly as I ran towards him, swinging the bat wildly. I caught him off guard, the bat connected with the side of his head. His body dropped to the ground instantly. Biggs laid on his back, with the little dignity he had left he tried to reach for something. I kicked him as hard as I could between his legs, he cried in pain while holding his dick. "I knew I'd catch you slippin' one day Biggs, ain't that what my mama Zora used to call you?" Biggs eyes shot wide open, he looked at me like I was crazy. Blood poured from the gash on his head, making him look even more intimidating. "I was only 5 you nasty bitch," I yelled, while hitting him three more times with everything I had left in me, tears began pouring from my eyes. Biggs tried to stand up, but I hit him once again with the bat. He laid unconscious, barely breathing from being beat in the head with a metal bat. "Your a fucking pervert, you fat sloppy piece of shit." I cried while standing over his body. Spitting out my razor, I slit his throat. Blood squirted from his neck, as a few splatters got on my clothes. Even though I knew he was dead for good measures, I pulled his pants down. It took me about 20 minutes to slice his dick off, once I got it off I shoved it in his mouth. "Choke on that, bitch!" I made my way from the alley and jumped into my car. I sped off into the night feeling good as fuck. For over 13 years, I always wanted to kill that mothafucka.

CHAPTER 12
Memory Lane

Cruising down Northwest 63rd street, I decided to take a trip down memory lane to my raggedy ass childhood. I haven't been back on this side of town since I was thirteen. I haven't seen Zora in over 3 years, I hated her ass with a passion and I was going to make sure she knew that. While I was in the area I wanted to check up on Kevin, to see if his business picked up. I just had a funny feeling, that taking this ride, wouldn't be such a good idea.

Everyone was outside, kids were playing in the streets and adults were drinking on their porches. Nothing changed about Pork and beans project, it looked so worn down it was sad. Looking at my old house, I felt saddened. Zoe took his last breath on that porch, my life would be forever tarnished because of that damn house. I sat there staring at the house, for over twenty minutes. In reality, I wanted to knock on the door and hoped Zora would answer. A part of me wanted to kill her, another part of me just wanted answers that I knew even she wouldn't give me. I just wanted to know why, why she hated me so much, why did she let all that shit happen to me. I wanted her to hug me and for her to tell me, she was sorry. I also wanted to slice her throat, while watching her take her last breath slowly and painfully.

As I was about to pull off, I glanced in my rear-view mirror. To my surprise, Zora was walking hand and hand with a handsome older guy. He had to be in his late forties, but he looked decent and well kept. Zora pranced by his side, with a huge smile across her face. She looked like she was happy and that pissed me off, I wanted her to be suffering right now. Instead she was out here living her best life, like she deserved it. Her hair looked old, but what stood out was her light brown skin, it almost seemed so flawless. It looked as if she gained some weight, she wasn't as curvy but she still had it a little. Her once plum and perfect JLo booty, looked like it had seen better days. I wondered if she cleaned herself up, or if she was still a controlled addict. Even when she was smoking, you could never really tell if you were just going by her appearance. Zora wore her famous blonde hair, but instead of the expensive bundles she used to get she had on a cheaply made synthetic wig. She wore black leggings, with a red blouse and black sandals. I watched them both, as they walked happily to her apartment. The man she was with kissed her and opened the door for her. After he walked off, he went towards the parking lot and got into an older model Ford Focus. It was obvious he wasn't rich, but it looked like he had his shit together. I made a mental note of him, placing it in the back of my mind. One day I would need him, he would be the biggest pawn in this deadly game against Zora.

I made my way to Kevin's shop, hoping he didn't mind me just popping up. I have never been to his shop before, so this unexpected visit shouldn't bother him I thought. I parked my car in someone's reserved spot and headed inside.

"Thank you for stopping at KK automotive, is there something I can assist you with?" A young girl asked me, while sitting behind the counter. I looked her over briefly, for some reason I couldn't stop staring at her.

"Ma'am, can I help you?" she asked once again.

"Oh, I'm sorry. Is Kevin available?"

"Yes, just give me one moment," she said as she stood up and walked towards the back of the building. She was a beautiful white girl, she had blue eyes and long blonde hair. You would think we were related, especially with my blue contacts in. I thought I was looking at myself for a moment when I looked at her, it was crazy how much we resemble each other. The only difference was, she was shorter than me and she also didn't have much of a figure, you could tell she was straight up white. But besides those few characteristics, we could pass for sisters. We both looked around the same age also, it was crazy how some of our features were exactly the same. Once she walked back to her desk, she informed me Kevin would be right out.

Almost twenty minutes passed before Kevin came out, along with two other females who stood on each side. Kevin's eyes widened when he saw me, it didn't look like he was too happy either. "Hello Rayne, give me a minute and I'll be right with you." He acknowledged my presence, while he walked both girls outside. They made small talk before I saw him kiss both of them on the mouth, before they got into their car. My heart started racing, I didn't know if I should cause a scene or handle it like an adult. I jumped up and ran outside, the girls in the car were already pulling off. "What the fuck was that Kevin?" Kevin just looked at me like he was trying to make up a lie. "Rayne just calm down; I do way too much for you, so don't come here acting like it's the other way around." "Furthermore, I don't have to answer to you or anyone." He began walking back towards the building, but not before I jumped in front of him and slapped him. Kevin grabbed me and restrained my arms, he picked me up and carried me inside. He threw me over his shoulder like a rag doll, I punched him repeatedly on his back like a toddler throwing a tantrum. My head swung left to right, as we made our way past the girl sitting at the front desk, our eyes locked immediately and you could tell she wanted to beat my ass, Kevin was probably fucking her too I thought.

Once we got into his office he slammed his door and locked it, he wasted no time getting undressed. "You want some attention? Well, I'm all yours now." After he got undressed he grabbed my arm forcefully, while snatching off my shirt and pulling the rest of my clothing off. He positioned me on his lap, while he sat in the chair. His dick was hard already, so he slid it right inside of me. Thrusting his hips back and forth on the chair, he dug deeper inside of me with each stroke. "I think you need some of this good dick to make you behave," he whispered in my ear. Loud moans escaped my mouth, I played with my clit looking at his dick going in and out of me. "Ugh, fuck this pussy daddy!" I moaned dramatically, while still riding him. "Yes, that shit feels so good." I bounced my ass all over his dick making sure to be a little extra, I wanted his secretary to get in on the action. Kevin started smacking my ass, watching it giggle from the back must have turned him on. We haven't fucked, since I got my ass and boobs done. "I'm cumming" he yelped, as he jumped up from the chair. As soon as I got down on my knees, he let his load off all over my face and breast. Grabbing my left titty, he sucked on it for a few minutes. "Don't ever bring your ass down here again," he said seriously, as he bit down hard on my nipple.

I got all my stuff together and got dressed, using his handkerchief to wipe his sticky seimen off of me. Kevin gave me a wad of money, rolled up with a rubber band around it. In my head, I calculated about $2,500. Giving Kevin a quick peck on his cheek, I made my way out of his office. Walking past the chick behind the counter felt a little awkward, since she looked at me with disgust written all over her face. "Duh bitch, can I help you?" I mumbled while walking past her, making sure to put extra switches in my walk. "There is nothing you would ever be able to help me with." She spat back, while rolling her eyes. "Good, because your man just gave me all the help I needed," I replied as I continued to walk towards the exit. The girl just laughed hysterically before she replied with a simple, "whatever."

I left the shop and drove right back towards Zora house. I noticed her porch light was on, she sat on the porch in an old chair with the same guy I saw her with earlier. He must have gone to the store when I saw him leave, because they were both drinking. They looked like they were engaging in a deep conversation, I sat across the street studying them both before pulling off.

Moments later, my phone went off. Looking down at the screen, a private number was calling me. Just like the other times, I let it ring out and go straight to voicemail. I didn't want anything to do with unknown numbers, it could have been the police for all I knew. Blasting my music to whatever was on the radio, I headed home.

I knew it would be hard seeing the projects today, my heart was still extremely heavy and I never got a chance to heal. I just wish Zoe was here, my heart ached for him. I knew he wouldn't approve of my doings, but I know he was happy I got revenge for him. Tears filled my eyes and made their way slowly down my cheeks. I knew this life I was living would be trouble, but I still didn't care. I would leave a mark on Miami, before my own untimely demise. Everybody would know who Heavenly was, I was going to make sure of it.

CHAPTER 13
Better Days

"**B**itch, you too good for me now?" Kacey yelled on the opposite end of the phone. "It's a white bitch out here killing folks and you're just ignoring my calls. "You're starting to make me think you're the serial killer." Kacey laughed, but I didn't like how she said that shit. "Bitch please, if I was the killer your ass would be dead too," I shot back. "Stop playing Rayne, come scoop me up. I turned all my tricks today; I need to get out of this room." She whined. "Alright, I'll be there in a minute." I told her, while ending the call.

Kacey's words replayed in my head; I knew she wasn't serious about me being the killer. However, it rubbed me the wrong way because I was the killer. I never really thought about being caught, that never crossed my mind.

I made my way to my closet, picking out an outfit for the day. Looking over my new wardrobe, I had to smile. It felt like it was just yesterday, when I didn't have shit to call my own. I was just a dirty ass girl, with one outfit and a pair of sneakers to my name. Now, no one could tell me shit. I decided to wear a blue crop top, with black shorts and blue tie up sandals. I put my hair in a tight ponytail with a flipped bang. I put on my gold jumbo hoops, and grabbed my black Alexander Wang handbag. Making my way out the door I sent Kacey a text, to let her know I was on the way.

Kacey was standing outside when I pulled up, she hopped in before I came to a complete stop. "Damn bitch, you're real desperate," I laughed. "Shut up Rayne, I hate being alone for too long." She turned the music up and we both danced in our seats, as City girls blasted through the speakers. Kacey was a die hard Cardi B fanatic. Personally, I didn't care too much for music at all. Today we would just ride out since we didn't have a destination, maybe this is all I needed.

Kacey and I engaged in small talk, while we cruised the city. She gave me an update on her personal life, her tricks and her money. I told her about the incident with me and Kevin, she was ready to beat a bitch ass too. I came clean last year and let her know he wasn't really my uncle, I thought she caught on by then anyhow. I told her to chill about the whole Kevin situation, because as long as he continued to lace my pockets I didn't care what he did, I just had to act like I did. After riding for over an hour, I begin to feel dizzy. My stomach started cramping, and I started feeling nauseous.

"Rayne, you alright?" Kacey asked, sensing something was wrong. "Yeah, I think so."

"Maybe I'm just car sick, I haven't driven this long before."

"Well bitch, you better man the fuck up, we in the middle of nowhere, and I damn sure can't drive."

"Shut the fuck up Kacey, you ain't making shit better," I snapped. Kacey rolled her eyes, reaching for her purse in the backseat she took out a blunt. "I no weed works wonder's, plus this some fire so hopefully it helps." Kacey rolled up and lit the blunt. After puffing two times, she started coughing and passed it to me. Taking two hits, I started gagging. I pulled the car over on the side of the road, a sharp pain shot up my stomach causing me to yell out in pain. "Oh my god Rayne, are you alright?"

Opening my car door I threw up, just missing the inside of my car. Looking on the ground, thick blood was mixed in with my vomit. "Hand me a napkin, it's in the glove compartment," I informed her. Kacey handed me the napkins; I wiped my mouth before throwing the napkin on the ground. "You want to stay at the motel?" Kacey asked with a worried expression on her face. "Nah, I'm good. I just probably need some rest, I haven't had much sleep."

The drive to the motel seemed like forever. I never felt like this before, all I wanted to do was lay down. Once we reached the motel, Kacey looked at me sympathetically. "Girl, go lay down and make sure you keep me posted." Kacey hugged me and got out of the car.

As soon as I left, I headed right to the drug store. I tried my best to look normal, but my body was sore as hell. I purchased three pregnancy tests, two bottles of NyQuil and some other flu medicine. I was hoping it was a stomach bug, I sure as hell didn't want no kid.

Once I stepped foot into my condo, I ripped everything off. I went straight for the bathroom and opened one of the pregnancy tests. Sitting down on the toilet, I pissed on the stick. Placing it on the sink, I sat and waited for the results. A single red line appeared on the stick, I looked at the back of the box, to see what that line meant. I was relieved when I compared the lines, I wasn't pregnant. Saving the other two tests, I placed them in the cabinet. If I was pregnant I'd be just like Zora and wouldn't know who my kid father was. The last thing I wanted was to be anything like her ass, she was the fuking devil.

I laid across my bed in drastic pain, it was so unbearable all I could do was cry. As much as I wanted to front, I was really in need of some real love. The sad part was, I didn't even know what true love was. I curled up in my bed, closed my eyes and silently prayed for better days.

Months went by and my condition worsened, I was still bed-ridden and unable to eat much. It got so bad that I allowed Kacey to stay with me. One rule we had was, no tricks allowed. I gave her a spare key, so she was able to come and go as she pleased. Even though Kacey was a big help, she had her days were I just wanted to tell her to get the fuck out. That was just the type of relationship we had; she was like a little sister I never had. In all actuality I was only a couple months older than her, but she didn't know that.

"Rayne, you need to go to the doctors." Kacey said, as she handed me some soup. "If this doesn't pass by tomorrow, I think I will," I told her.

"Bitch, you've been sick for over three months, something ain't right," she fussed. "I know Kacey, I think I have a bad case of food poisoning." "You lost mad weight, you look pale as fuck, whatever it is, it's beating your ass." I nodded my head agreeing with her, so she could shut up. I knew something was wrong, but I was scared to find out what it was. I didn't know if it was the injections for my ass, or if it was something more serious. Kacey was right, I looked horrible.

"Kacey, call me an uber please." I asked her, my voice was barely above a whisper. I really wanted to call Kevin, but I decided against it. Since the incident at his shop, he's been dodging me lately. "Alright, I'm going with you." Kacey called out from the kitchen. "No,

I'm fine you stay here. I'm a big girl, I can handle myself."

"Bitch, haven't you heard of the Uber killer?" Kacey yelled again. She was giving me a damn headache, her over dramatic ass was always yelling and overly paranoid. Ignoring her, I gathered my belongings. "So, you really don't want me to go?" "I'm serious Rayne, people have been murdered fucking with them Uber drivers."

"People have also been murdered for fucking with me," I said seriously. Kacey just looked at me like I was crazy, she moved out of my way as I reached for the door and gave me a hug. "You better call me," she warned. "I'll call you later Kacey, don't worry about me" I assured her.

I sat in the emergency room, for over six hours. My blood was drawn, my temperature was taken and I was hooked up to an IV. The young brunette nurse checked on me constantly, she said I was severely dehydrated. All they were waiting for now were my lab results. I didn't have the flu or any other stomach virus, so now they wanted to find out if I had any STD's. Kacey called me every hour, making sure I was alright. Once I got some fluids in my body, I started to feel a little better.

Finally, a male doctor walked in accompanied by the same nurse who's been checking on me. "Hello Mrs. Boykins, my name is doctor Campbell." The doctor was Jamaican, with a deep seductive accent. He had neat dreads, but his dark chocolate skin looked so smooth and perfect. The doctor continued speaking, addressing me by a fake name I gave once again. "We have your lab results, I need to know how long you have been experiencing this pain?"

"Maybe about three months," I told him. He nodded his head, while he wrote something down on his pad. "Unfortunately, ma'am your HIV positive." The doctor continued to talk, telling me how sorry he was and how I can still live with the virus since they caught it in the early stages. Whatever else he was saying after that; I couldn't even tell you. I tried ripping the IV out my arm, I started kicking and screaming with no remorse for any other ill person in the hospital. About five nurses tried to restrain me, but no one could calm me down. Eventually they gave me a sedative and I could feel myself drifting away. It was right in that moment when I realized, there was no such thing as better days.

CHAPTER 14
Livin' To Die

Waking up in S5, was the result of me trying to kill myself. If it wasn't for the stupid ass janitor, my suicide attempt would have been successful. Once I got the news that I was HIV positive, I completely lost it. I didn't want to live, when I was just livin to die. After the doctors restraincd mc they took me to the 10th floor, that was basically where they put sick people. After five minutes of being on that floor, listening to the cries, the moans and all the people in pain, I had enough. Taking a chair, I bust out the window. A loud shatter, echoed throughout the entire floor. "Grab her!" Was all I heard, before taking my leap to death. I took a deep breath and jumped; however, I never reached the ground. A male janitor rushed to grab me, as he yelled for help. He held on to both of my wrists, his grip was tight and he refused to let me go. My entire body was hanging from the window, dangling from the 10th floor. I tried to wiggle and scratch him, praying he would drop me but he didn't. A nurse came to his aide and together they pulled me back inside. My room was packed with every nurse on the floor, even the other patients flooded my room. They immediately transferred me to S5, where I am now.

My weight dropped dramatically again; I went from 162 pounds to 105 pounds. My shape was looking horrible, the surgery only made it look worse. In all reality, I fell into depression. Being in S5 only made it worse, I just wanted to go home. Kacey was blowing my phone up daily, once I finally answered she let me hear it. I was all kinds of inconsiderate bitches; she was mad as hell and she made sure I knew how she felt. She even came to the hospital, they told her they had no one by the name of Rayne Shine since I gave my fake name and that only infuriated her more. I felt bad because I really grew to love Kacey, but I was hiding so much from her. My phone buzzed, letting me know I had an incoming call. Technically I wasn't supposed to have a phone, but I refused to let them keep my shit. Looking at the caller ID, Kacey was calling me back. "Yes Kacey," I answered with an attitude.

"Rayne, I just want to see you. I'm sorry for all the shit I said, but I haven't talked to you in three weeks. I've been going crazy, worried sick about your ass." Kacey cried into the phone; I knew that she authentically cared for me but I didn't know how to accept it. "Alright, they put me in S5 because I was going crazy. I'm at Mercy hospital, my room number is 543." We ended the call and I prepared myself for Kacey's arrival.

Almost an hour went by, before Kacey waltz right into my room. She had balloons and flowers in her hand. Making her way to my bedside, she placed everything on my stand. Once she took a look at me, she burst into tears. "All I want is to be here for you Rayne, why won't you let me?"

"Oh wait, your name ain't even Rayne, right?" Kacey asked, as she sat down on the chair, next to my bed.

I could see the love Kacey had for me, truth is I really didn't know how to love her back. I could feel in my heart that I loved her, but it was hard expressing it. I took a few deep breaths before responding, she deserved to know the truth. "Listen Kacey, I'm not who you think I am."

"Well that's obvious," she replied sarcastically while cutting me off. Rolling my eyes at her, I continued. "I've been living in hell, since I was born. I witnessed my brother die when I was 5, my mama sold me for drugs. Once I got to high school, I was bullied. I never experienced love before, so I know I'm a little rough around the edges."

"A little?" Kacey interrupted again. Ignoring her, I continued because I didn't want anything to stop me from telling her the truth. "After today, you may not want anything to do with me." Kacey looked at me with tears in her eyes, "don't say that shit Rayne."

"Kacey, I said that to say this. When you came here, they told you there wasn't a Rayne Shine here. That's because I always use an alias, but that's also not my real name. I've changed my appearance so much that no one was able to recognize me, not even you."

"Okay, now you're freaking me out." "Before I go into all that I want you to know, I'm still in this hospital because I'm HIV positive." Kacey looked at me dumbfounded, with her mouth wide open. "I'm so sorry Rayne," she said as she sobbed in the chair next to my bed. "Listen Kacey, I know I'm going to die but I want to get something off my chest."

"You're not going to die, you can beat this shit," her voice was filled with so much determination that I almost believed her. "I'm pretty sure you'd want me dead, if I told you my name is Heavenly."

"Get the fuck out of here" Kacey said while looking at me in disbelief. "You mean Heavenly from high school?" I shook my head yes, as tears fell from my eyes. "Damn Heavenly, all these years I never fucking knew." Kacey still looked at me, as she tried to register all of this. "I still love you like a sister, that doesn't change shit," Kacey replied. "I have a question though, why befriend me if you hated me?"

"I didn't really hate you, I just hated how you let Saharra control you. To be honest with you, I was supposed to kill your ass too but I grew attached to you," I told her. "You're not serious right now Rayne, I mean Heavenly," Kacey said as she corrected herself.

"Yes, I'm being dead ass serious."

"I don't care about that old shit Heavenly, I really just want you to get better, I just want to be that special person you never had." I burst into tears, my emotions were all over the place and no one has ever shown me they cared for me as much as Kacey did. Kacey stood up and bent down to hug me. "What's wrong Heavenly, is there something else you need to tell me and what the fuck you mean kill me too?" Kacey asked, realizing I had a hidden agenda this entire time. I wiped my tears, and looked her dead in her eyes. "You might want to get tested, we slept with the same people. Even though mine was unwillingly, we still had a common sex partner."

"Who Heavenly? I'm so lost right now, can you stop going in circles and tell me what the hell is going on?" Kacey was getting agitated, her entire demeanor changed almost instantly.

"Calm down Kacey and lower your voice."

"Don't tell me to calm down, tell me what the fuck your talking about," she spat. I began explaining everything to her, hoping she'd believe me. "Dom and his friends raped me, they gave me two STD's but one was treatable. They humiliated me, sodomized me and beat me. They left me for dead, like I was road kill or some shit. I eventually killed them all for what they did to me." "When I saw you that day at the motel, my whole purpose of inviting you into my room was to get close to you, before killing you. I wanted to pay you back for how you treated me in school." Kacey rocked back and forth in the chair, tears pouring from her eyes. "I'm so sorry they did that to you, why didn't you tell the police?" Kacey asked. I didn't answer her question. "Heavenly, I wasn't fucking Dom. We started as close friends; we just started dating a week prior to his death. He always wanted to fuck me, but I never let him because he was a grown ass man."

"I'm happy you killed them sick bastards, if I would have known I would have helped you, because that's what a true fucking friend would do." Kacey stopped talking, she then looked at me and you could tell she was broken inside. "I guess I was the only true friend here; you were just a bitch trying to get revenge." Kacey's words hurt, but she had all rights to be upset. "I'm so sorry Kacey, I didn't hurt you because I grew to love you," I told her. "Love me? You know what, fuck you Heavenly. I didn't deserve this shit, I know you've been through a lot but that doesn't mean it's okay to just go around hurting people and pretending to care about them."

"I love you like a sister, so before I say some shit I shouldn't, I'm just going to leave." Kacey stood up, and walked out the room without saying anything else. "Kacey, wait" I yelled. My voice cracked, as I called out for her. I cried non-stop, until a nurse walked in to check my vitals. "I think you need your medication," she whispered. "Fuck you, you fat sloppy ass bitch," I yelled. She immediately called for help, two other nurses entered my room and they held me down, as the fat bitch stuck me with a needle. I started kicking as hard as I could, but then the medicine caught up to me. My eyes felt heavy and I felt lifeless. Before I knew it, I was out.

Days turned into weeks; weeks turned into months. Kacey wasn't answering any of my calls and Kevin was out of town. I was finally transferred to a regular floor, since I was no longer considered a risk to myself or others. I was taking my medicine regularly and I started counseling. I also managed to gain twenty pounds back. Talking to people who were HIV positive helped me a lot. Hearing some of their stories gave me a glimpse of hope. Some of them have been HIV positive for over ten years, while some were just recently exposed to the virus. I wasn't even 20 yet, I didn't want to die. Someone in the group I was attending asked a question that stuck with me, the lady said, "what is the point of living, when we all are just living to die." And I felt that.

Two weeks after I was transferred from S5, I was released from the hospital. I was given information on HIV and how to live with it, since I would have this disease for the rest of my life I had to make sure to treat it properly. If it ever turned into AIDS, I knew my chances of survival were slim. I was taking ART, which was Antiretroviral therapy. As long as I took them every day, without any fuck ups I should be fine. I took an Uber home from the hospital; I didn't know what to expect when I got home. It's been almost five months, since I've been there. Once I got inside, I could tell Kacey cleaned before she left. I gave her an extra key, so I wasn't sure if she had been here recently. I was kind of hoping she was here, it was so much I wanted to tell her. I knew she was mad at me, but I really needed her right now. Her phone was going straight to voicemail, that shit really bothered me. Hopefully one day she would find it in her heart to forgive me, but for now I was going to roll a fat blunt and forget about everything. Kacey has been nothing but a loyal friend to me, I was determined to get to that back.

CHAPTER 15
Deadly Combination

"Kacey please call me back, I'm really worried about you." I ended the call, leaving yet another voicemail. Two months have passed, I still haven't talked to her. I've been in the house, getting my weight back up. I was now 128 pounds. Eating junk and smoking was doing my body justice. I also did light workouts, to maintain my figure. I talked to Kevin a few times, he wanted to come over sometime next week when he got back into town. I was kind of happy he wasn't around; I wouldn't know how to break the news to him. The fucked-up part about it was, I wasn't going to tell him. It really didn't matter because he probably already had it too, who knows he was probably the one who passed that shit to me.

Today was the day that I decided to get up and get out. I picked out a cute little two-piece jumpsuit, with the matching hat. It was a little chilly outside, since it was late February. I wore an army fatigue jumpsuit, with brown Timbs.

My hair grew back so long and full, it reached to the middle of my back now. I put my hair up in a ponytail so that I could put my hat on, I wasn't a hat person but the whole outfit was cute. I put on some mink lashes and fix my eyebrows. Dabbing into my makeup, I mixed colors that went with my outfit. Once my face was beat, I added black lipstick. I walked out of the house with one thing on my mind, finding my next victim.

Blasting my radio, I drove through the town with malice intent. Stopping at the liquor store on NE 1st Ave, I made my way inside to grab some Henny. After purchasing my bottle, I made my way back outside. "Hey, aren't you Kacey's friend?" I heard a familiar voice ask. Turning around, I saw Chaz standing nearby. He had a big smile plastered across his face, waiting for me to respond back to him. "Yeah, that would be me. Do I know you?" I looked at him like I didn't recognize him. Chaz walked over to me, he started to explain how he knew me. Of course, I played along. "What are you doing over this way, you're a long way from home aren't you?" I asked him playfully. Chaz and I talked for a little while, before I got into my car. He went into the liquor store, while I waited for him to come out. "You need a ride?" I asked, as he walked out of the store. "I mean it wouldn't hurt," he said as he climbed into the passenger seat. We rode around town for over an hour, before I told him I had to stop at a motel.

"What are you getting a room for?" he inquired. "I just want to relax by myself, I've had a rough week." "Girl, your sexy ass should never be alone do you mind if I join you?"

"Don't you have a girl at home?" I asked him, knowing damn well I didn't care.

"Saharra will be alright, "I won't tell if you won't," he laughed. Hearing her name made me cringe. My plan was working, all I had to do now was fuck him and send him right back to her ass.

"Damn Rayne, this pussy good as fuck," Chaz moaned. We had been fucking for over a half hour. Once I purchased the room, it didn't take long for us to start taking off each other's clothes. Chaz wanted to use a condom, so I had to think of something quick. He started off by licking my pussy, then he inserted his pencil dick inside of me. "You want to suck my dick?"

Chaz asked, as he pulled his dick out of me. At first, I wanted to decline his offer but this was my only opportunity. Getting on my knees, I took off his condom, I slurped and sucked for all of two minutes. Standing up, I pushed him on the bed. Positing myself between his legs, I started sucking his dick again. Before he could object, I jumped right on his hard wood and put him inside of me. "Wait, what happened to the condom?" Chaz asked, confused.

"I'm clean, I hope you are?" I questioned. "Yeah, I'm clean too." Chaz wanted to hit it from the back, so I got up and let him take over. His dick was whack as fuck; I faked an orgasm two times. I was hoping by faking he would have got his nut off, but it only turned him on more. "Fuck me Chaz, fuck me," I moaned like I was getting some A1 dick. "Matter of fact, put it in my ass," I ordered him. Anal was never my thing, but I knew HIV was much riskier through anal. That hyped him up even more, he started pulling my hair and smacking my ass. His pumps got faster and I could tell he was about to climax. "I never knew your ass was this freaky," he said out of breath. I clapped my ass on his dick, while playing with my pussy. If his dick couldn't make me cum, I knew my fingers would. "Ugh fuck, where do you want me to put it? Chaz asked, as he pumped faster.

"Put that shit all over my ass," I told him. He made a funny grunting noise, then he pulled out. Jerking his dick, he let his nut drip all over my ass. Once he was done, he collapsed on the bed. Even though his sex was trash, I was happy that my plan worked. I knew he would go back and fuck Saharra, they would both suffer how I wanted them to. A smile crossed my face and all I wanted was for him to leave.

"Oh shit, my boyfriend is on the way, Chaz you have to go." Chaz jumped up from the bed, running around getting his shit together. "Damn, why didn't you tell me you were expecting company?"

"I wasn't, he just texted me out of the blue, somebody told him my car was at this motel." Chaz got his shit and headed for the door, "That was some good pussy, I hope I can get it again." Without responding, I closed the door on him.

After he left, I hopped right in the shower. No one was coming here; I didn't even have a damn boyfriend. Chaz didn't need to know that though, I just wanted him gone. My ass was burning from the anal sex, so I sat on the toilet and took a shit. When I wiped myself, blood covered the toilet paper. That made me feel even better, anal fucking and blood was a deadly combination, hopefully it worked as planned. Standing in the shower, I lathered soap on a rag. Washing my body, I was hoping I was able to pass the HIV to him. My mind wouldn't let me stop thinking if he didn't get it, then the entire fuck was pointless. I didn't feel an ounce of remorse, I was actually happy that he and Saharra would die slowly.

Gathering all of my belongings, I left the motel. My phone started buzzing, letting me know I had a text. I opened my phone, surprised as Kacey's name popped up. **"I'm okay Heavenly and I hope you are too. I just need some time to think, I'll always love you. Sisters 4 life xoxo."** I was happy she texted me, even though we left off on bad terms I knew she wouldn't be able to stay away from me too long. I didn't bother sending her a message back, I sat my phone on the seat and headed home.

Pulling into my driveway, I was surprised to see Kevin's car. From the looks of it, he was already inside. I fixed my lipstick and made my way inside.

"Hey Rayne, you're looking fabulous as always." Kevin greeted me, as soon as I stepped foot in the door. "Thank you, baby," I replied as I kissed his cheek. Kevin rubbed his dick up against me, letting me know he was ready for some pussy. "I don't want the toys this time, let me just get some of that good pussy." Kevin said, letting me know he wanted to skip the foreplay and that was fine by me. Kevin sat down on the sofa in the living room, I made my way over to him undressing along the way. "You missed daddy's dick?" he asked. "Of course, I've missed daddy's dick," I replied seductively. Kevin must have had a troubling vacation, he sure was taking it out on my pussy. He pounded my walls hard, then he ate my ass and fucked me again. For over an hour, we fucked hardcore. He didn't slow down until he was about to climax, this time he didn't pull out. Kevin emptied his load inside of me, he kissed me on the forehead and headed towards the bathroom.

"I'm going to shower, I have to head back to the shop." Kevin called out. I made my way upstairs, to take a shower also. I knew he wasn't going to the shop, he was a player but he made sure I was good. No matter how many bitches he had, I would also be number one. In my heart I kind of felt bad for Kevin, I had feelings for him but I knew he would contract HIV also. I felt guilty, but I shut those feelings out. It could have been him who gave it to me in the first place, even though I doubted it I never put shit past anyone. If I was going to die, I was taking everybody I could with me. I didn't have time to be feeling bad for people, since people never felt bad for Heavenly.

CHAPTER 16
Nobody's Safe

*F*or the past month, I've been stalking Zora and her man. She may have thought she got away with what she did to me, but I was coming for that ass. I found out her man name is Andre. He worked as a cook at the Holiday Inn, on his lunch break he would do a light workout in the gym at the hotel. He seemed like he was all into Zora, but I knew any nigga would fall for some pussy. Zora was washed the fuck up, I'm pretty sure her walls were non-existent. I fucked a lot, but I also did Kegel exercise. Once he got a feel of this tight pussy, he wouldn't be able to resist it. I was growing impatient, I wanted to make a move on him as soon as possible. However, I wanted to make sure I didn't fuck up my plan by rushing it.

Walking up to the front desk, I purchased a room. "Thank you for choosing Holiday Inn, we hope you enjoy your stay." The front desk clerk said, as I paid for my room for three nights. "Is the gym included in my stay?"

Yes ma'am, it sure is," she replied with a smile. I had all the information I needed, I walked off smiling carrying my gym bag and headed up to my room. Once I got settled I'd be making my way to the gym, in hopes of seeing Andre.

The first night staying at the hotel, I went to the gym at 8:15 pm. This was usually around the time I would see Andre working out, but today he wasn't there. I walked the treadmill, played with the dumb bells, but he still didn't show up. Around 9:30 pm, I left the gym and headed back to my room. Taking a quick shower, I ordered room service hoping he would be the one to deliver my food. Room service came, but there was still no Andre. I was getting frustrated, I stalked this man for weeks just to learn his schedule. Now that I put my plan into effect, he was nowhere to be found. The food I ordered was untouched, I didn't even have an appetite anymore. I went to bed angry, hoping tomorrow I'd catch my prey.

"Oh, shit baby, your fucking me so good." Loud moans and the sound of abusive fucking awoke me. Whoever was in the room next to me, was getting fucked like they stole something. I tried to cover my ears with pillows, but it seemed like the chick screamed even louder. Pounding on the wall, I yelled for them to shut up. "It's 3 o'clock in the morning, you fucking morons."

"Well, find you some dick bitch," the man yelled back. All I could do was laugh, if he only knew I was trying to find some dick but it was nowhere to be found. Since I had no other choice but to listen to them fucking, I used it to my advantage. Instead of being mad, I played with my pussy. My body trembled in just a few minutes, from the explosive orgasm I just had. Once my juices poured from my pussy, I fell back to sleep.

Waking up the next morning, I felt refreshed. Hopping in the shower, I decided to get dressed for the gym. With only a few items to choose from, since I thought my plan would work the first night, I opt for a two-piece spandex outfit. I threw on some track sneakers, to match my outfit and did a once over in the mirror. I sat in the room flicking through channels, trying to refrain from boredom. I ordered some alcoholic beverages through room service. Moments after placing my order, I heard a deep voice say "Room service," while knocking at the door. Looking through the peephole, my heart damn near skipped a beat.

Opening up the door, Andre walked right in. He rolled a tray in with two glasses, with my champagne sitting in a bucket of ice. "Why would room service think I need two glasses?" "Not everyone has someone," I snapped.

"I'm sorry ma'am, I can take the other glass back," Andre replied politely. "No, it's fine. I'll just feel the glass up for the imaginary person who will drink with me," I said sarcastically. I put on such a show, I was crying and being overly dramatic. "Ma'am are you ok?" He asked, showing concern as he placed his hand on my shoulder. Wiping my tears, I looked at him briefly. "Would you mind joining me? I literally have no one, I lost everything when I moved to the states," I lied.

"Well, unfortunately I'm on the clock but if you give me a half hour, I'll be back." As soon as he left, I took off my clothing. I wanted to set the mood and look provocative. Spraying my body with glitter perfume, I decided to wear a pink nightie. Standing in front of the mirror, I smiled at my enticing figure. I put on light makeup, and wrapped my hair in a bun.

An hour went by, before I heard a light knock at the door. I didn't want to seem too excited, so I took my time.

"I'm sorry it took so long, I had to finish up in the kitchen," Andre replied apologetically as I let him inside. "Don't worry about it, I was just about to commit suicide," I said jokingly. "Don't say that, you're too beautiful for that nonsense. By the way, you look lovely," he complimented me as his eyes wandered over my body.

"What's your name?" I asked him, acting as if I had no clue.

"My name is Andre and yours?"

"My name is Rayne. I'm assuming since you came back, you don't have a woman at home waiting for you?"

"Nah, not at all, I'm single." He replied without hesitation.

See that's why I hated niggas; all they do was fucking lie. I knew for a fact he was fucking Zora, wasn't no man gone spend that much time with a bitch, without getting some pussy. I also knew Zora didn't have anything in that house, that would make him think I was her daughter, so his lies were unnecessary. She never in her life took any pictures of me, not even when I was a baby. I knew for sure he didn't know who I was, but I knew who the fuck he was.

"Are you alright?" he asked politely, snapping me out of my thoughts.

"Oh, I'm fine. I just don't see how a handsome man like yourself is single." After engaging in small talk, he walked over to the Champagne he brought earlier and popped the bottle. Andre poured us both a glass and we continued our conversation. After the third glass of wine, I was feeling myself. I started dancing in circles, while rubbing all over my body. Moments later, Andre joined me. His dick poked me in my ass, from the feel of it he was packing. Making a bold move, I dropped to my knees and removed his pants. I Thought that he would object, but instead he started taking off his shirt. With his wood in my mouth, light moans of pleasure filled the room. I was working my magic on his full-size shaft, deep throating him while playing with my pussy. The wetness of my own pussy, made me stroke his dick ferociously. Without notice, he lifted me up and placed me on the bed. Bending over doggy style, he licked my pussy from the back. Once he was done, he quickly inserted himself inside of me. Looking back at him I could see his toes curl, giving me indication that he was enjoying my sweetness. Sweat poured from his head, as he eased in and out of me. I was happy he didn't ask to use a condom, that made it so much easier for me.

"Damn baby, this pussy is so good." Andre cooed, as he continued to pound my insides. "If the pussy is good, can you imagine what the ass feels like?" I asked him. He opened his eyes quickly. "You want me to put it in your ass?" he asked, seeming a little hesitant. "Hell yeah, just lube it before you put all of that in me."

Andre grabbed some oil off the stand, I sat it there purposely before he arrived. He took advantage of this anal opportunity, you could tell he wasn't use to it. His entire stroke changed and within minutes he released himself inside of me.

We both made our way to the bathroom, cleaning ourselves from the love making we just had. Once we were done, we both laid in the bed naked. Andre wrapped his arms around me, as we sat in silence. Shortly after he fell asleep. Instead of joining him, I placed all of my belongings inside my bag, took all of his money out of his pockets and left the room like a thief in the night, leaving no trace of my presence.

CHAPTER 17
See You In Hell

"**K**acey you no you still have a key to the house, come home whenever you want."

I was talking to Kacey on the phone, since I told her the truth about me last year, she has still been kind of distant. Even though she was still trying to build her trust with me, we were now back to communicating on a daily basis. It took us over three months to start talking again. "Awe Heavenly, I love you so much girl, but I'm trying to stand on my own two feet," she replied. Kacey had fell on hard times, her money was slowing down and she was tired of fucking for money. I didn't mind if she came to stay with me, but she was just so stubborn. She has been living out of that motel for over five years, I didn't want her living like that anymore. "Listen Kacey, I know we have had our differences but I'm concerned about you, if you refuse to come stay with me at least let me help you find a place," I offered. "It's alright Heavenly, I'll be ok for the time being."

We finished our conversation and ended the call. I can honestly say, I really missed Kacey.

After hanging up with her, I got dressed for the day. I decided since it was a bit warm, I'd wear a dress. Picking out a multicolored Gucci dress that went right above my knees, I wore green Gucci sandals to match. I used edge control to lay down my edge and swooped my hair into a high ponytail. Grabbing my green and red Gucci handbag, I headed out the door.

Before I could get into my car, my phone started ringing. I just hung up with Kacey, so I was confused why she was calling back. "What's up K," I answered. "Heavenly, I just got a call from Saharra, Chaz died two days ago." Her voice was shaky, it sounded like she had been crying for hours. "Damn, I'm so sorry for your loss, I know y'all was really close. Would you like me to come pick you up?"

"Heavenly, he died of complications due to AIDS."

"What? Aids? So, all this time it was him, he fucking gave me that shit?" I began fake crying into the phone. "You had sex with him?" Kacey was surprised to hear that, I knew it caught her off guard so I didn't answer her. "Maybe all this time it was him she continued, Saharra has been sick for about five months now, he passed it to her as well."

"Chaz had sickle cell, so when they diagnosed him with HIV, they knew his body wouldn't be able to fight it off and it turned to Aids quickly."

"You know what's crazy K, I only fucked him to get back at Saharra. That night I came to the motel, you asked me to give them both a ride, that same night we fucked." "Now look, I'm the one who's going to die, all because of revenge," I sobbed into the phone like a pro.

"I'm here if you need me girl, I'm so sorry." Kacey apologized over and over, it was obvious she didn't know that I really passed it to his ass. "The funeral is tomorrow, I'm going to show my face since Chaz was like a brother to me."

"Well, I'll go with you, despite how I feel right now, you know in high school I was head over heels with that boy. I'm hurt, but I need closure."

"I understand, well pick me up and we can go together," Kacey said. "Alright, I'll be there early," I told her before we ended the call. Placing my phone on the seat, I burst out in laughter. I deserved an Oscar, because I was a hell of an actor. Hearing Chaz died and Saharra was suffering, made me feel like I was accomplishing something. As sick as it sounds, I felt good about it.

Instead of cruising to look for my next victim, I decided to go back into the house. I wanted to pick out an outfit for the funeral tomorrow. Even though Chaz's death was sooner than I expected, I was hoping it was Saharra who would have died first.

Rolling a blunt, I laid across my bed butt ass naked. Tomorrow couldn't come fast enough.

Waking up at 6 in the morning due to Kevin texting me, put me in a shitty mood. I was getting tired of his ass, for the past three months he's been really distant and he was barley around. The amount of money he was giving me was decreasing. I think he was going through a financial hardship, so he took his frustration out on me. Keeping Zoe's advice on saving money was doing me justice, even if Kevin put me out today I had enough money saved to get my own shit. **"We need to talk ASAP,"** was the text I got from him. I texted him back, **"I have a funeral to go to today,**

maybe another day." He never responded back. I was up now, there would be no way I'd be able to go back to sleep. Making my way to the bathroom, I took a nice warm shower. My tears mixed with the water, as I broke down and sobbed like a baby waiting to be fed. Sometimes I had my moments where crying actually helped. I know I could be doing so much better for myself, but unfortunately I let the sins of my mother curse me. Wiping my face, I washed up and got out of the shower. If you looked at me, you would never be able to tell that I just had a breakdown moments ago. One thing about me, I was good at suppressing my emotions.

"I'll be ready in twenty minutes." A text came to my phone, from Kacey. She was letting me know she'd be ready soon. The ride to the motel was only ten minutes, so I had to get myself together. I went with a knee high, black dress. Some black heels and gold accessories. My hair was straight, since I flat ironed it already. I put on light makeup and wore lip gloss, my look was plain but cute. Locking up, I left the house. I Sent a text to Kacey to let her know I was on the way.

Me and Kacey made our way inside of Plymouth Congregational Church where Chaz's funeral was being held, not too many were in attendance though. Kacey wanted to sit towards the front, but I preferred to sit in the back. "C'mon Heavenly, it's not that many people here we can move closer." Kacey grabbed my hand and we made our way closer towards the front. A girl sitting in a wheelchair caught my attention. "Oh my God, Saharra looks awful, I feel so bad I haven't been there for her" Kacey whispered. It took everything in me not to burst into one of my famous laughs. Saharra looked almost unrecognizable, her once flawless complexion was now covered with blotches. She was very thin; her hair was wrapped up in a scarf. Inside I was rejoicing, but on the outside I had to keep calm. Kacey went over to give Saharra a hug, they talked briefly before she came back to sit down next to me. A woman went up to the podium, she addressed herself as Chaz's mother. She spoke highly of Chaz, then offered other's the opportunity to speak. Saharra was the first one up there, her mother wheeled her to the front. Once she was done, Kacey got up and said a few words. The funeral ended, with the pastor preaching. When it was time to view the body, Saharra burst into tears. I made my way up to his casket to say my goodbyes, he looked like he was at peace. He wore a black suit, his hair was cut really low, but the makeup they put on him was a bit excessive. Of course they wanted to hide his condition, but it was just too much. "Bye, bye, bitch!" I whispered.

"I'm going to the bathroom, I'll be right back." Kacey said, with tears in her eyes. Glancing around the church, Saharra was sitting off to the side by herself. I made my way over to her and gave her my condolences. Looking up at me, she smiled slightly as she nodded her head weakly. "Your Kacey's friend Rayne, right?" she asked, barely above a whisper. Smiling at her I replied, "I'm her best friend and your worst enemy." I bent down a little further so that what I was about to say, would only be heard by the two of us. "If I took out these fake ass contacts, changed my hair color to honey blonde and had on dirty clothes, do you know who I would be?" Saharra looked up at me again, "just a dirty bitch," she replied with no emotion at all. Taking a step back, I let out a gut-wrenching laugh. "Nah, I'd be the bitch who's responsible for your man's death, as well as yours. I'm completely satisfied, that you're dying slowly and in severe pain." The look on Saharra's face, turned into pure discomfort. "I'm Heavenly, now do you remember me?" Saharra looked around frantically, by her facial expression you could tell she was shocked. "Well, I have to go for now but I'll see you in Hell bitch." Winking my eye at her, I made my way towards the exit. Kacey said her goodbyes to everyone, then made her way outside as well. "Are you alright?" Kacey asked, as she got into the car. "I'm great," I smiled. Turning up the radio, I sped off. I was finally getting sweet revenge on all the mothafuckas who did me wrong. It felt good seeing each of them suffer, but I wasn't quite finished yet.

CHAPTER 18
My Next Victim

"**A**re you trying to go to the club tonight? It's supposed to be lit," I asked Kacey.

"Nah boo I can't, I have to get this money." We were talking on the phone but Kacey was moving too much, so it was hard to hear her. "What the fuck you doing K, are you fucking?" "Yes bitch, I am." "My needs aren't going to pay for themselves," she chuckled. "Damn, you could have told me instead of fucking in my ear. Call me later nasty," I said while ending the call.

STORY Nightclub was packed as hell, cars were lined up all the way down the block. When I finally found a parking spot, I knew it would be a long haul in heels up the block. Slipping my razor in my bra, I got out of the car and made my way to the club. I was looking fly as ever, I was definitely feeling myself. I was rocking a fire red Coco Chanel skin tight dress, that was one size too small. My black stilettos, tied up my legs and hugged my calfs. I had a red Chanel clutch, with diamond hoops in my ear. My hair had just been pressed, less than an hour ago. I dyed it back to its original color, honey blonde/brown. My ass was bouncing out of my dress, causing me to get almost too much attention from the partygoers. Making my way to the front of the line, I handed the bouncer my VIP pass. "That dress looks real good on you." The bouncer said, as I made my way inside the club. I gave him a wink, before disappearing into the crowd. Heading straight to the bar, I got me a henny and coke. Before I could purchase my drink, someone placed money on the counter. "Her drinks are on me," a familiar voice said. Looking behind me, Andre was standing there. I took a big gulp of my drink, hoping he wouldn't cause a scene. "That's kind of fucked up how you did me, I should have known your young pretty ass was shady." Andre practically yelled in my ear, trying to make sure I heard him over the music. "I know you ain't mad over that little ass chump change."

"It's the principal." Andre said, as he ordered himself another drink. "So why are you spending money on me now? I mean, you did get some pussy right?" He just laughed, ignoring my questions. I didn't have time for this shit, I was trying to find my next victim, since he was already one of my victims I really didn't want to be bothered.

The beat for Juvenile back that ass up burst through the speakers. The crowd went wild, so I made my way to the dance floor. No matter how old that song is, that shit never gets old. Dancing with a random guy, I popped my ass all over him. He was feeling up my dress, but I didn't even put up a fight. I began twerking, as he fingered my pussy. "Meet me in the bathroom, in twenty minutes." I whispered in the guy's ear, before going back to the bar. Andre was nowhere to be found, so I placed another order. Let me get three double shots of Henny, I told the bartender. Several dudes came up to me, trying to get my attention. I told all three of them, to meet me in the bathroom. I knew by the time I met them there, it would be at least five of them. I was targeting innocent people, which I knew was wrong. However, at this point I didn't even care because all niggas are the same in my eyes.

Taking shots of Henny had me feeling tipsy and in my own zone. My vibes were on a different level, I was feeling myself way too much. Glancing throughout the club, I started to see the men making their way towards the bathroom. They were coming from different directions, hopefully they would all play nice. I took one more shot and headed to the back of the club. Once I got to the men's room, the five men were waiting for me. "What the fuck y'all here for? This was supposed to be a private party," one of them shouted. "Yeah, so why the fuck you here?" Another one yelled back. "Listen here guy's, I invited all of you. If y'all can't stop acting like a bunch of bitches, I can just excuse myself."

Each of them looked at one another, debating if they should stay. "Get at me when you're alone, I ain't got time for this shit, one of them said as he barged out the door.

"Then there were four," I chuckled playfully. In front of me was one light skin dude, one dark skin, and two Mexican twins. At first, I was just going to go with the twins, then I got a little greedy. I locked the door and began undressing. All four men were unbuckling their pants. Getting on my knees, I opened my mouth for one of the twins. The other twin laid on the floor, so I got on top of him and inserted his dick into my awaiting death trap. Everyone took turns, changing positions occasionally. "Damn ma, this pussy fire," the dark skin dude moaned. If only he knew this type of fire was not going to go out, I thought.

Once all four of them were ready to climax, I sat right in the middle of them as they formed a circle around me. Each of them began jerking swiftly until they reached their peak, my face was dripping bodily fluids from four complete strangers.

"Alright, get the fuck out," I snapped. Each of them looked at me like I was crazy, "Y'all heard what the fuck I said right?"

"You're a crazy bitch," the light skinned dude mumbled. "You know this is the men's bathroom, right?" one of the twins interjected. "I don't give a fuck, just get out," I yelled again. All four of them got dressed and scurried out the bathroom, I quickly locked the door behind them. Cleaning myself up, I smiled in the mirror. A light tap on the door, snapped me out of my trance. Unlocking the door, I attempted to leave the bathroom. "You mine as well let me hit, you done fucked the whole club," an all too familiar voice said." Looking up, Andre was standing behind me. "Boy fuck you, get out of my way." I told him, as I tried to bypass him. Grabbing me by my throat, he pushed me back inside. "I'm going to show you how hoes get treated," he scoffed. Andre started fidgeting with his zipper, his eyes were glossy. Looking at him, I could tell he was high as fuck. That's the same look Zora used to have, when she finished snorting. Rushing towards me, he attempted to grab my neck again. This time I was prepared, so I jumped to the side. He caught the front of my dress, ripping it slightly. I wasn't expecting this from him, he seemed like the perfect gentleman. I guess that cocaine can do that shit to you. Once he regained his balance, he tried to attack me again. Grabbing my razor out of my bra, I swung it recklessly. At this point I didn't care where I sliced him, I was putting up a fight for my life. I guess the cuts didn't faze him, he still continued to charge me. "Bitch, you gone give me some pussy," He grumbled. I knew now, just how powerful pussy was. I robbed this man and left without a word and all he wanted was some more pussy. Blood trickled into his eye, blinding his vision temporarily. I took that as my que, to pounce on him. Kicking him in his nuts, he dropped to his knees in agony. I kicked him in his throat, as he fell on his back. Standing over him, he winced in pain. I knelt down, bringing my razor across his throat. He made gurgling sounds, as he tried to apply pressure on the wound. I watched him fighting for air, but the blood was choking him. Once he took his last breath, I washed my hands and flushed the razor, leaving him lying on the bathroom floor. Instead of going through the crowd, I dipped out of the back entrance. Once I got to my car, I sat there and rolled a blunt. I couldn't believe I almost became a victim, trying to find my next victim.

CHAPTER 19
Death Bed Confession

"**R**eporting live from STORY nightclub on Collins Ave, right here in Miami Florida. After a night of partying, the owner of this prestigious nightclub, found a deceased male in his club bathroom. As of right now, no suspects have been named. We will update you, when more information becomes available."

Watching the news, I couldn't help but let out a sigh. I could only imagine how the owner felt, looking at his beautifully buffed floors covered in blood. Andre deserved what he got; he had the audacity to try to take advantage of me. Turning off the TV, I turned my phone off. Kevin was blowing me up nonstop, all he kept saying was he needed to talk to me. If he wanted to talk that bad, he would have just come by. It wasn't like he didn't have the key, so I continued to ignore him. Making my way to the kitchen, I whipped up a quick sandwich. After eating, I jumped in the shower. I didn't have any plans for the day, but I decided to get dressed, just in case Kacey called me. She was good for last minute plans, but I always enjoyed her company. Speaking of Kacey, I turned my phone back on, knowing she would worry herself if I didn't answer. My phone started vibrating, letting me know I had a missed call. Looking through the call log, I missed two calls from a blocked number. A voicemail notification showed in the upper right corner of my phone; my heart dropped immediately because the other private numbers never left a message. Fearing it was a call about my HIV status, I listened to the voicemail.

"Mrs. Shine, This is Doctor McDaniel's, contacting you from Jackson Memorial Hospital. You're listed as next of kin, for a Mrs. Zora Shine, it's very important that you come in as soon as possible, thank you." After listening to the voicemail, I was relieved. I was happy it wasn't my doctor calling to inform me of a change in my status. What I didn't understand was how they got my number, or why Zora had me listed on anything. A part of me wanted to say fuck her, but the other part wanted to find out what was going on. Making my way into my bedroom, I threw on a jogging suit with matching sneakers. Tying my hair back into a ponytail, I left the house.

Once I arrived at the hospital, I made my way to the front desk. I've been using the name Rayne or an alias for so long, I was skeptical to give them my real name but I did anyway. After checking in, a nurse walked me to the elevators, letting me know Zora's room number was on the visiting pass. Once I got off the elevator, I took a deep breath. My mind told me to leave, but my feet continued to walk towards her room. Peaking my head into her room, I was appalled when I saw her. She was hooked up to several monitors, with an oxygen tube in her nose. Her face was sunken and she didn't have her wig on. "Hello, are you Heavenly?" A soft voice startled me, as I stood outside of Zora's door.

"Yes, that would be me," I replied.

"My name is Dr. McDaniels, I reached out to you regarding Mrs. Shine." I nodded my head, while shaking the doctor's hand. "What is your exact relation to Mrs. Shine, if you don't mind me asking?" "I'm her estranged daughter," I murmured. The doctor filled me in on Zora's condition, letting me no she didn't have much longer to live. Zora has been admitted for over a month now, with no sign of progression. She had AIDS and she was also fighting breast cancer. They tried to get the AIDS under control, but since her body was so weak and she waited so long to get treatment, there was nothing they could do. Her immune system shut down, leaving her in the current state she's in now. Just looking at her, tickled me inside. I did everything I could to keep a straight face in front of the doctor, little did he know I didn't give a fuck about this bitch.

I was directed to put on a face mask and gloves, it was proper protocol for the hospital to ensure visitors were safe.

The doctor excused himself, so I made my way inside the room. Sitting beside Zora, I just looked at her frail body. Hours went by and I found myself dozing off. "Heavenly?" I heard a light whisper, but I could have sworn I was dreaming. Then I heard it again, "Heavenly is that you?" I damn near jumped out of the chair, I looked right at Zora. Her eyes were merely open, but I could tell she was awake.

"I've been looking all over for you, but I could never find you." Zora whispered. "I'm sorry for being a horrible mother, it was nothing but the drugs. I was focused on my next fix, instead of you. The drugs ruined me, but I've cleaned up babygirl." "Before I die, I just want you to know I love you. After everything I put you through, you still came here to see about me."

Zora looked at me in shock, when I burst into laughter. The look of sorrow was written all over her face. "Bitch you're crazy, if you think I came up here to make amends with you. I came up here to make sure you are actually dying. I hate you; you ruined my life purposely." Fighting my tears, I continued to spit venom at Zora. All the anger I had built up, was finally coming out. "Before I leave, I just want you to know I'm happy your sick ass is dying." "Oh, and Just so you know, I know you and Max killed Zoe, now I'll be responsible for killing your grimy ass." Zora looked at me confused, tears falling down her cheeks. "I gave your boyfriend HIV, I fucked him knowing he would go back and give it to you. But don't worry, you won't see him anymore either. You fucked up my life, took my brother's life, now I'm taking yours."

I grabbed my purse, so I could leave. "Heavenly, I just want you to know one thing." Zora stopped me right in my tracks, I was hoping she wouldn't say she loved me again, then I'd really have to end her life. Zora began speaking, realizing she got my attention. "You always wanted to know who your daddy is, I promised myself I would never tell you or anyone else. Since I'm dying, I want you to try to find him and reconcile your relationship with him."

"Now you want to tell me who my daddy is? You're a bird ass bitch for real," I shouted.

"Despite how you feel about me, at least contact your daddy. He is the owner of KK automotive, right by Pork and Bean projects." My heart felt like it was going to jump out of my chest, it felt like everything around me was spinning. I was hoping she was just bullshitting, but before I could ask her, she started coughing violently. Her monitors started going off, causing several nurses to run into her room. Taking one last look at Zora, I knew that would probably be her last breath. I turned to walk out of the room, not knowing what to do. She had some nerve telling me who my daddy is, after all of this time. Running into the bathroom, I threw up everything in my stomach. I couldn't believe who she was claiming to be my dad, that shit couldn't be right. Zora's death bed confession cut me to the core. A part of me wanted to go back to her room, I wanted to kill her myself. My eyes were red and puffy, I dabbed cold water on my face and headed out the bathroom. I walked out of the hospital, with my head hung low. Tears danced in the corner of my eyes, as I tried to hold it all together. My life was officially ruined, by the same person who gave birth to me. I couldn't believe how all my pain was always connected to Zora. I didn't feel like going home yet, so I would go find comfort in Kacey. I started feeling sick to my stomach again, this time I could have sworn I felt little flutters or kicks, but I pushed that thought to the back of my mind. What could I possibly do, I was too ashamed and embarrassed to tell Kacey about this. I would have felt better not knowing who my daddy was, instead I've been fucking him and calling him daddy all this time.

CHAPTER 20
Up in Flames

"*G*irl, my world is falling apart. You don't even know the half K, maybe one day I'll fill you in." I was talking to Kacey while walking in circles, I've been staying at the motel with her for the past week. I brought most of my belongings, as well as the money I've been saving. I kept it at the motel, just in case I had any trouble with Kevin.

Two days ago I got a phone call, letting me know Zora passed. I was happy the bitch was dead, but I still left to pick up all the pieces to this mysterious puzzle she left behind. Kacey was trying to get me to open up, but I was too embarrassed to even speak on those skeletons. "Everything will be alright Heavenly, you're a strong ass bitch." Kacey said playfully. That was the first time I smiled, since leaving the hospital. Kacey just had a way of making me feel good, she was a true friend. For some reason, I was afraid to go home. Since leaving the hospital, I felt like I was being watched. I could have been paranoid, but my gut feeling told me otherwise.

"C'mon Heavenly, let's go for a ride. You've been inside this motel for days, let's go get some air." I couldn't help but to agree with Kacey, so I made my way to the bathroom to freshen up. I threw on some Nike jogging pants and a tank top, Kacey threw on something similar and we left out. Before I got into my car, I scanned up and down the street, making sure I wasn't being watched. "Why are you being so paranoid, Heavenly? You act like you're wanted for murder or some shit." Shrugging my shoulders, I started up the car and drove off. We rode around with no particular destination, stopping to grab an ice cream cone, we sat and talked outside the parlor. "You want to go to this after party with me tonight?"

"You and these parties Heavenly, now you know I hate the party scenes. I'm not into that type of crowd, I'm too laid back for all the hype," Kacey replied.

"It's nothing wrong with having some fun, maybe you need to give that pussy a break." I laughed. "Fuck you, this pussy keeps me fed, with money in my pocket." I may not be rich, but I'm living. So, don't try to play me."

"Girl, calm down ain't nobody trying to play you, I was just fuckin with you." I told her sensitive ass. We continued eating our ice cream, talking about our future and what we wanted to do with ourselves. Out of the corner of my eye, I could have sworn I saw Kevin's car drive by. "You good?" Kacey asked, noticing the change in my mood. "Yeah, I'm fine, are you ready to go?" Kacey nodded her head and we left.

I drove back to the motel to drop Kacey off, I had too much on my mind and all I wanted was a stiff drink. I still haven't called Kevin back and I didn't plan on it either. "Are you still going to the party? You seem a little hesitant, maybe you should skip this one."

"Nah, I'll be fine, I need to get out. Plus, it's my birthday weekend." I knew Kacey had good intentions, but I had to turn up. I turned legal yesterday, even though my driver's license says I'm 25. Today would be the day that I would celebrate my birthday, since it was a Friday.

"I'm worried about you Heavenly, but I know you can hold your own. Make sure you call me, so I don't have to come find you." Me and Kacey embraced in a hug, before she got out of the car. We said our goodbyes and I pulled off. Making my way home, I still felt uneasy. I should have called Kevin back, but a part of me was scared. How could I face a man, who could potentially be my father? In my heart, I felt Zora was fucking with my head, but what if she wasn't? What if the man I've been with was really my father?

Once I got in the house, I went straight for the fridge to Grab a bottle of Hennessey. Pouring me a shot, I gulped it down expeditiously. Tonight was an event for an upcoming rap artist. I would be sure to make my appearance known, especially with my outfit. It was in the mid 70's, the weather was perfect for my open toed stilettos. Getting dressed, I decided to wear all black. I wore a black one piece, skin tight, pant suit. My hair was curly and I put more makeup on than usual. I wore a silver body chain, with silver hoops. Looking in the mirror, I sprayed on some perfume and danced slowly. Tonight I just wanted to enjoy my birthday, I didn't want to taste revenge. I left the house already feeling tipsy and ready to party, I never thought I'd see 21.

"Kiki do you love me? Are you riding? Say you'll never ever leave from beside me." Drake's, in my feelings blasted through the club speakers. Everyone on the dance floor was turnt up. The crowd was definitely showing out, with some of the top artists in the building. I ordered myself a henny and coke, sipping it slowly while vibing to the music. "Hey beautiful, do you mind if I join you." A handsome, tall guy said as he approached me. Any other time I'd be interested, but tonight I just wanted to chill. "Nah, I'm good. Maybe another time," I told him. His ego was bruised, but at least he dodged a bruised dick. In all actuality, his sexy ass just sent a wave of electricity up to my pussy. My wet box started twitching, as soon as I laid eyes on him. His slim body, full beard and beautiful white teeth did something to me. Throughout the night, I was approached quite a few times. I turned down all of them, including the club owner. My phone started vibrating, letting me know I had an incoming call. Looking at the caller ID, it was Kacey calling me. I answered, but the music was so loud, I could barely understand what she was saying. "I'll call you when I leave," I yelled into the phone. After ending the call she called back, I let it ring out. It was already past 2 am, I knew it would be hell to get out once the party was over. I got one more drink and sipped it slow before leaving.

Making it home safe, I immediately stripped. Taking off the club wear, I ran a nice cool bath in the bathroom downstairs. Turning on some music, I danced in the full-length mirror. I was drunk as hell, but I felt good. It just dawned on me that I haven't returned Kacey's call, I ran to my room and searched for my phone but I couldn't find it. I was already naked, so I wasn't too thrilled about running to the car to see if my phone was in there. I wrapped myself in a bathrobe and made my way to the front door.

"Are you going somewhere?" I jumped back, almost falling flat on my ass. I regained my composure, as Kevin stood outside my door. "What the fuck Kevin, you scared the fuck out of me." "All I asked was, if you're going anywhere?" He replied, with a sly grin. I didn't know what to think, as he stood there looking at me. His hands were behind his back and he wasn't dressed like he normally would. Kevin was never seen wearing nothing less than suits and ties, instead he stood before me wearing a sweat suit with basketball sneakers. My heart felt like it skipped a few beats, but I stayed calm.

"I see someone is too good to answer my calls now?" Kevin smirked. "Nah, not at all. I've just been really busy lately," I told him. "Busy?" he burst into laughter, which made me feel a little uneasy. "Busy doing what, Heavenly?" I couldn't believe he called me by my real name, now I knew something was up. I contemplated my next move in my head, but the liquor clouded my judgement.

"Don't look so surprised, I've been doing a lot of research on you." Kevin stopped talking while looking me over, then he continued again. "I was wondering why there were no records of anyone by the name of Rayne. Then I had my daughter look into it, come to find out there is no fucking Rayne."

"That got me thinking, why would a beautiful young girl like yourself lie to me? What would be the purpose, so I started following you. I followed you to the hospital, where you visited that bitch Zora. The same bitch who extorted money from me, since the day you were born."

"What the fuck are you talking about Kevin?"

"Don't be so naive, you know exactly what I'm talking about. Your mother always claimed; I was your daddy. We fucked way back in the day and she used you as a pawn. I gave her monthly payments for a kid who is not mine, just so she wouldn't ruin my marriage, but she still did."

"Kevin I really didn't know; she would never tell me who my father was. I grew up not knowing, me and Zora were never close, I just found all this out a few days ago."

Kevin started laughing again, "you're a good liar, just like your mother. Both of you bitches played me, like mother like daughter," he yelled.

I was getting aggravated standing in my doorway, listening to him rant about shit I had no clue about. Kevin thought he knew what he was talking about, but it was far from the truth. If only he knew, me and Zora never got along, the bitch hated me just as much as I hated her.

But he wasn't going to listen to me, he thought he had everything figured out.

"Well, since your mother is dead, I think it's best that you join her." Kevin smirked, as he threw a clear liquid substance on me.

"What the fuck is that?" I screamed, as my eyes started burning. The smell was so strong, I damn near passed out. I tried to form a coherent sentence, but nothing would come out. I tried running to get a hold of something to wipe whatever he shot on me, off of me.

"I could never be responsible for creating something like you." "You and your mother picked the wrong guy, now you'll pay for your mother's sins." Kevin sparked a match and threw it at me, my entire bathrobe went up in flames. All I heard was the door slam shut, I ran around screaming, as the flames engulfed my body. Everything I bumped into, caught on fire. I was trying so hard to put the fire out, the more I tried the more the fire spread rapidly. I finally ran towards the bathroom and jumped into the tub of water that I was running before Kevin came. My skin was burning, the pain was intolerable. My entire condo was up in flames, the smoke was so thick nothing was visible.

The smoke felt like it was suffocating me, I felt myself fighting for air which was almost impossible. I didn't make it this far in life, just to lay down and die. With everything I had left in me, I fought through the flames.Wood creaking and electricity crackling could be heard, just before my entire condo went up in flames.

CHAPTER 21
Shoulda Killed Me

1 couldn't stop the tears from falling, I cried while watching the news. I laid wrapped in bandages, from my feet to my stomach. I drove myself to the hospital, making up some dumb ass story about why I was covered in burns. Once I arrived, I was taken to ICU. The pain from the burns didn't amount to the pain I felt in my heart. On the news was a picture of what used to be my home. What hurt the most was the headline, which read.

An unidentified female remains found in suspicious fire.

I knew Kevin was happy, thinking that was me. But it wasn't me. He was going to wish it was me though. I've been in the hospital for two days now; it wasn't until yesterday that I checked my phone. Kevin sent me several text messages, before he appeared at my front door. What had me in tears, was the voicemail Kacey left me. I replayed it over and over again, she sounded so happy. The voicemail she left for me said:

"Hey boo, I'm on my way to your house. I just finished up with my last client and I made a hella tip. I'll be stopping by the liquor store, so I can grab a drink. I know your ass will be drunk by the time you get home, so I will be too. You know I got the key, so I'll see you when you get in. Oh, I bought you something special for your birthday, I hope you like it. I love you Heavenly Rayne, Sisters 4 Lyfe!!"

Every time I listened to her, I cried nonstop. My best friend was dead, all because of me. Kacey was all I had; I couldn't believe she was gone. If I would have known she was upstairs sleep, I would have tried my damndest to save her. I was so distraught; I didn't know how to feel. I was so hurt that Kacey had to die like that. She was such a sweet person; she didn't deserve that shit. I wanted so desperately to find Kevin. My mind wouldn't let me rest, as I thought of so many ways to kill him.

The nurses thought my tears were due to the pain from the burns, so they continued to dope me up with meds. I had 3rd degree burns on my foot and legs, 2nd degree burns covered my thighs and all the way up to my stomach. It was a miracle; my face didn't catch fire.

A light tap startled me and a chubby black nurse walked into my room. "Hello honey, I know you're in a lot of pain but we will be getting you ready for surgery." "The surgeon will be conducting a skin graft, to cover up the 3rd degree burns."

"Also, your urine test came back, you're 3 weeks pregnant." Once the nurse finished talking, I closed my eyes. I wasn't trying to be rude, but I wasn't thinking about no damn baby. All I wanted to do was get better. Once I was able to get out of here, I'd fix all of my flaws. I already had plans of changing my appearance again, I left all my stuff at the motel. I knew it would be hard going back to the same motel Kacey lived, but I had no other option. Just thinking about going there and Kacey not being there, made me emotional once again. All I know is, Kevin fucked up. He should have killed me, now I would haunt him until I made him suffer, like he made an innocent Kacey suffer.

CHAPTER 22
Hell in ATL

Many things changed within the past few months, including me. Everytime I look in the mirror, it's a constant reminder of how I almost lost my life. Even with the skin graft, the burns were still conspicuous. I may not have been able to hide the burns, but I was able to conceal them. I never went back for prenatal care and to be honest, I didn't even feel pregnant, nor was I showing.

I went to a tanning booth faithfully, at least 3 times a week to change my skin tone. It was against the doctors orders, but I didn't care. I was now 2 shades darker than my usual color. I dyed my hair jet black with red highlights and I wore grey contacts instead of blue or green.

No matter how much I tried to occupy myself, I always found myself thinking about Kacey. Her parents gave her a private funeral, with only about 20 people in attendance. I can honestly say, they slayed my girl. Her burns were covered by concealer, she looked beautiful and at peace. The corner said she would have made it, if she didn't inhale so much smoke. Her body wasn't burned as much as her lungs were. I laid in the motel room reminiscing about all the times we shared, I promised Kacey that I would get revenge for her.

I was one step ahead of Kevin, whether he knew it or not. I traded in the car he bought me, for an all black BMW.

I sat outside of his house that he shared with his wife, watching his every move. I was aware of his daily routines, from the time he woke until the time he went to sleep I knew where he was and what he was doing. I had a plan for Kevin, but that came to a hult when a U-Haul pulled into his driveway. Looking at the license plate, the truck was from Atlanta. I wasn't expecting this, so I had to think of something quick. Without thinking, I hopped out of my car and made my way to the truck. Tapping the driver side window lightly, I was able to get the drivers attention.

"Can I help you? " he asked.

"Can you tell me where you're moving these folks to?" He looked at me skeptical at first, until I peeled off a couple hundreds from my pocket. His face lit up and I knew he'd be willing to do whatever I asked. "I'm moving them to Buckhead, right on Collier road." "Would you happen to have the address." I quizzed? He grabbed a piece of paper and jotted down something quickly, he handed it to me and told me that's the address for delivery. I handed him $500 more and walked back to my car. "Can I at least get your number shorty?" He called out after me, but I ignored him and got inside my car. I sat there for a few minutes, observing what he scribbled on the paper. I was praying he didn't fuck me over, I needed this more than anything. Moments later, Kevin walked out of his house and sped off in his car. I gave it a few minutes and I pulled off also, it wasn't necessary to follow him anymore, so I made my way back to the hotel. As soon as I got back to my room, I began packing. ATL wouldn't be ready for the hell I was going to cause, I was going to show up and show the fuck out.

Weeks passed by rather quickly, I was living in a motel room roughly five minutes from Kevin's new home in Atlanta.

I was able to learn his schedule just by watching him daily, I also found out he had another business here.

I sat outside of their home and watched as Kevin's wife brought luggage to her truck, Kevin helped her load up her belongings. I assumed she was going on some kind of trip, since the luggage was a bit excessive. I've been in Atlanta for about 3 weeks now, I was getting homesick and ready to put an end to Kevin. I wondered if Kevin was HIV positive since we had unprotected sex, he never mentioned it before he tried to claim my life. I sat there taking him all in, he didn't look any different and he didn't look like a man who was capable ofmurder. He still looked like the clean, well-kept business man that I was used to seeing. Kevin kept the secretary from KK Automotive, I've seen her quite a few times leaving the house. I never knew anyone who dealt with their secretary outside of business hours, I just knew he was getting a piece of that cookie.

My black car didn't look suspicious parked in this upscale neighborhood, almost everyone on the block owned some kind of black sports car or foreign car including Kevin. Tonight, I made up in my mind that I would make a move on Kevin. I've been stalking him long enough to know that he would be home by midnight, he would go upstairs and undress for the shower, he'd grab one of those overly expensive robes to put on after and watch tv for a bit. His secretary wouldn't be there tonight, but she usually got to the house around 9 am the next morning. I knew everything about this man, but he didn't even know that I still existed.

Once everyone went their own ways, I left the area to grab something to eat. My stomach continued with the weird flutters, I tried to ignore them anytime I felt it which was usually often. I wasn't prepared to have something growing inside of me, I didn't even know how to be a woman, let alone a mother.

Around 11pm I parked my car 2 blocks away, I walked to Kevin's house like I was an expected guess. I carried a black bag, with many surprises for Kevin. If I wasn't mistaken,

I knew he had a spare key under the plant on the porch, that would grant me easy access.

When I arrived at his house the key was exactly where I saw him put it, I unlocked the door and went inside. The house was beautiful, everything was furnished and color coordinated. I walked up the spiral staircase that led to the master bedroom and placed my bag under the bed. His wife's closet was filled to capacity with different types of clothing. I helped myself to a red nighty, I was sure she wouldn't mind.

After getting dressed I sprayed myself with body shimmer and fixed my damp hair. I didn't get a chance to blow dry it before I left the motel, so it was still a little wet.

At exactly midnight, Kevin pulled into the garage. I laid on the King sized bed, my burns were visible by the nightlight that stayed on in the room. I thought my plan through but I was very nervous, as I sat there anticipating his reaction. Kevin's footsteps could be heard coming up the stairs, he walked into the room and flicked on the light. "Who the hell are you? Why are you in my house?" Kevin's voice was a bit shaken, I faced the opposite direction so he didn't see my face. He also didn't pay attention to the burns that covered me from waist down. I turned around to face him and his face immediately turned pale. Gripping his chest, he stumbled against the wall. "Looks like you've seen a ghost Kevin, you might have just given yourself a heart attack," I laughed. "Your dead bitch, this can't be possible," he stuttered incoherently. "Well then, I must be a ghost." My dramatic laugh caused him to flinch, I grabbed the taser that I placed on the side of the bed. Kevin attempted to charge me but he was too late, two darts from the taser pierced his chest and he dropped to the floor stiff as a board.

"Why do you always have to play with people? Just kill the mothafucka."An unfamiliar female voice came from the hallway. I turned around hurriedly as his secretary stood by the door. "What the fuck are you doing here? You're not usually here at this time of night." I questioned. "I'm making sure you kill our father," she let out a light giggle like something was funny. "Our father, what do you mean our father?" Now I was getting mad, this bitch was confusing me.

"This piece of shit is your dad?"

"You mean **our** dad, sus." She corrected me.

"Since the day your ratchet ass walked into KK automotive, I knew we were sisters. Kevin had me do some research on you, I put 2 and 2 together and came up with you. Kevin wanted to deny it all, but he knew in his heart he was fucking his daughter and then tried to kill you so you wouldn't expose his nasty ass."

It was all starting to make sense now, Kevin always said I reminded him of someone, but he would never say who. "Let's put him on the bed, and by the way my name is Hellen, but everyone calls me HELL." She smiled deviously and walked towards Kevin, we put tape over his mouth and put him on the bed. "I guess we're about to give him some Heavenly Hell," she joked.

I really didn't find the shit funny, I didn't even know if I could trust her. I didn't really have a choice now, since she was already here. Hellen wore all black, with black gloves and boots on. If I didn't know any better, I would have thought she knew about my plan. I couldn't stop looking at her, she looked even more identical to me since she dyed her hair darker black like mine. "Are you going to admire my pretty ass, or are you going to help me?" she fussed. Kevin had one hand tied to the bed already, but he was squirming and it made it harder for her to tie his other hand. "Now get on top of him, so we can make it look like he was having an affair." "I'm going to snap some pictures, so just try to be sexy." She ordered. I didn't ask any questions, I just went along with her plan, since obviously mine was thrown out the window. She snapped several pictures before Kevin started squirming again, he was trying to speak but the tape wouldn't allow it.

"Pop, Pop!"

A bullet whizzed right past my ear and entered Kevin's forehead. "Damn bitch you could have warned me first, I wanted to kill this mothafucka for killing my best friend," I yelled. Hellen just ignored me, which only infuriated me more. I got off of Kevin, his eyes were rolled to the back of his head and blooded seeped from the bullet wound in his forehead. I had to change these clothes and get out of here, I'm pretty sure the neighbor's heard the gunshots. I reached down to grab my original clothing, but not before a blunt object pierced the back of my head. Reaching for the back of my head, I felt blood leaking and an oversized lump that put me on the verge of fainting. I dropped to my knees, unable to hold myself up. Hellen stood next to me holding the gun in her hand. "Why the fuck did you do that," I managed to slur. "Bitch I hate you, you may not no me but I know you." I just looked at her, as she continued to express her feelings for me. "You ruined my life and my family Heavenly, you and your psycho ass mother." "I'm only 10 months older than you, because my dad wanted to fuck greedy, money hungary black bitches."

"That white uppity bitch you call a mom ain't no better," I interjected.

"Your right about that, that's why she'll be going down for murder," Hellen laughed the same dramatic laugh that I did. We were so common in many different ways, the shit was actually sick.

"Kevin has never done shit for me, I had to work my ass off for everything I got." "Then here comes bitches like you, who get his time, attention and money for free. Shit started getting so bad in our household, I moved out on my own because my own mother started resenting me." You could see the hurt in Hellen's eyes, as she stood there and spoke about how much her life was ruined because of me. I was trying to make sense of everything, but with all the blood I was losing, I didn't know how much longer I could force myself to stay awake. "You made everything so easy Heavenly, you're too damn gullible and you trusted the wrong bitch." "Once the police get their hands on this double homicide, this neighborhood won't ever be the same."

"The story will go a little something like this." Hellen stood straight up like she was posing, she held her hand up towards her mouth like she was talking into a microphone. Her entire voice changed, as she pretended to be a news reporter. "**A wealthy businessman was tragically murdered by his wife Kimberly Koster. 44 years old Kevin Koster was brutally murdered when his wife walked in on him having an affair with his mistress. Both victims were pronounced dead at the** scene, his wife's whereabouts is currently unknown but it is expected that she has fled the country." "What do you think about that story, shit sounds official right?"

I just looked at Hellen like she was crazy, she was probably more sick than I was. She had everything planned out and it sounded almost too perfect. "My mom is a weak bitch, I held this family together and I'm going to inherit everything that is rightfully mine," she said. Hellen walked towards Kevin to untie him, I used that as an attempt to find something to knock this bitch out with. My mind was telling me to move, but my body wouldn't allow me. I was weak and I knew if I didn't get help I'd die. Since there were no other objects in sight, I jumped up as fast as my body would allow and ran for the stairs. "Bitch you must be stupid if you think I'm going to let you fuck shit up for me," Hellen was yelling now, she sounded completely different or more like demonic. I made it to the third step before I felt Hellen's boots connect with my back, I lost my balance and hit each step hard, as I rolled down them like a slinky. I felt paralyzed and that shit scared me, I wasn't able to move my legs and my arms felt like they were broken in a few places. "You always have to be so extra Heavenly, if you would have just stayed calm all of this could have been over by now." Hellen taunted, while standing over me. Hellen's words echoed in my head, I wanted to get up and fight but I couldn't. She stood over me but I didn't recognize her anymore, she looked demonic and her eyes were lifeless. My breathing began to get shallow, I was trying my damnedest to fight death. "I heard you like to use razors on your victims," Hellen whispered with a smirk on her face. She pulled a razor from her bra, like I often did.

"Your pathetic Heavenly, I'll see you in hell bitch."

"Wait, I'm preg...." My words were cut short when she lifted her hand swiftly and slashed my throat, I fought against the blood making it's way down my esophagus. Hellen stepped over me and disappeared, leaving me to fight for the life of me and my unborn child, whom I never wanted in the first place. Heavenly may have gotten revenge, but she was no match for Hell.

I laid there alone, scared and in pain as my life flashed before me. It was kind of crazy how I was leaving this world, the same way I came in.

A Word From The Author

Thank you, from the bottom of my heart for choosing this Novel to read. My purpose on writing Heavenly Revenge, was to shed light on Child abuse, rape, and molestation. I know it may be a lot to take in, but remember;everyone handles pain differently. Teach your children about bullying and also be a voice. I have a passion for spreading the word, on this type of abuse. If you want to know why I'm so passionate about it, please grab a copy of "This Life I Lived." It's my own personal story, of how I overcame being a victim of sexual abuse. I also have a nonprofit organization, called Speak Up and Live Inc. which reaches out to victims of abuse. If you SEE something, SAY something. #SPEAKUP You can find Speak up on Facebook also! Any question you have, please feel free to email me at Mrs.Author@myself.com